"I'm with Christopher now," Aisha said. "I don't have anything going on with Jeff. Besides, he undoubtedly has a new girlfriend. Probably several."

"Maybe at least one will be his own age this time," Mrs. Gray said darkly.

"Mother, I think I would like to see him play through. I mean, he's an old friend who's having his first big success. He wants to have all his old friends around to see him do well. It would be impolite to say no." Immediately Aisha winced. Wrong choice of words.

"Yes, you always did have a hard time saying *no* to Jeff Pullings, didn't you?"

"You know what I mean," Aisha said.

"And you know what I mean," her mother shot back.

Don't miss any of the books in
Making Out
by Katherine Applegate
from Avon Flare

Coming Soon

MAKING OUT #8

Aisha goes wild

KATHERINE APPLEGATE

Originally published as *Boyfriends Girlfriends*

AN AVON FLARE BOOK

Originally published by HarperPaperbacks as *Boyfriends Girlfriends*

AVON BOOKS, INC.
1350 Avenue of the Americas
New York, New York 10019

Copyright © 1994 by Daniel Weiss Associates, Inc., and
Katherine Applegate
Published by arrangement with Daniel Weiss Associates, Inc.
Visit our website at **http://www.AvonBooks.com**
Library of Congress Catalog Card Number: 98-93054
ISBN: 0-380-80219-8

First Avon Flare Printing: January 1999

AVON FLARE TRADEMARK REG. U.S. PAT. OFF. AND IN OTHER COUNTRIES, MARCA REGISTRADA, HECHO EN U.S.A.

Printed in the U.S.A.

WCD 10 9 8 7 6 5 4 3 2 1

For me to Michael.
And vice versa.

Benjamin struggled to his feet. He managed a swollen, misshapen smile and stuck his hand out in the general direction of Lara. "It's true, I am your half brother, and I'd really appreciate it if you didn't let your boyfriend kill me."

Lara stared at him closely. Keith was up again, mostly recovered. "You're blind, aren't you?" Lara said.

"Blind?" Keith grunted.

"Yep, I'm your blind half brother Benjamin. Later, if I'm still alive, I'll introduce you to your blond half sister Zoey."

"Think it through, Jake," Claire sneered. "You just told Zoey a lie about her boyfriend. You just told her Lucas slept with me. A lie. A pathetic lie you told because you wanted Zoey back. Think it through, Jake," she snapped, suddenly furious.

"I don't . . . You're the one who told me," Jake protested.

"Me?" Claire looked surprised. "Why on earth would I go around telling people I slept with a guy I'm not even seeing? Why would I tell a lie like that?" She put her face close to his. Her beautiful, cold-eyed face. "Whereas you, Jake . . . You would make up a lie like

1

that to get Zoey back. A low, contemptible trick to break up Zoey and Lucas, to take advantage of her vulnerability and get her to come back to you. How do you think Zoey will feel about you when she realizes you've done this to her, Jake?"

He looked at her in horror.

"You and Lucas," Claire said. "Both of you so in love with Zoey. What was I, Jake? What was I?"

Lucas ran, through random, quick-melting snowflakes, down the cobblestoned streets, plowing through the groups of fashionable, yuppie, restaurant-crowd types, around the rowdy college-age bar patrons.

The ferry's warning whistle sounded high and shrill. He ran full tilt, slipping on wet brick sidewalk, scrambling up, panting.

The ferry's whistle shrilled again. Too late, but he ran across the last street and slammed against the railing. The gangway was up and the ferry ropes cast off.

She was there, standing at the stern, looking down at him from her high perch.

"Zoey!" he cried out, rattling the railing in his frustration.

Her face was set in rigid lines of bitterness.

"Zoey, it isn't true!" he yelled. The ferry was pulling away, a dozen feet of water already between them.

Slowly and deliberately, Zoey turned her back and disappeared.

Zoey

Halloween is coming up soon, supposedly the time to be afraid. Or at least to think about fear. Or maybe it's just a time to wear masks and eat other people's candy.

You want to know what scares me? Not monsters. Not aliens. Not the guy from the movies, the guy with the long razor blade fingernails. What scares me are needles. I mean, when I have to go to the dentist, it's the novocaine needle that bothers me most. Lying there on your back, your mouth open with that little sucking thing hanging from your lip, a bright light in your eyes, carrying on a conversation where all you can say is "uh-huh, unh-unh" and a kind of yodeling sound that means "I don't

know." Then, up from no-
where comes the needle, float-
ing, hesitating, then
plunging right into your
gum. A needle. In your gum.
You want to scare me on Halloween, try dressing like a
dentist.

But you know, it's inter-
esting-to me the things that
end up being really awful in
my life aren't the things that
I'm scared of. The bad things
are the ones I didn't even see
coming. Like when Benjamin
lost his sight. Or like my
parents getting separated
recently. Or finding out that
Lucas...

Anyway.

Anyway, those have been the
really terrible things in my
life so far. None had much to
do with being scared.

You grow up as a kid
scared of the monster who

lives in your closet, or scared of the dark, or even like me, scared of the dentist. All that wasted fear, when it's just the day-to-day reality that ends up being awful.

One

Zoey Passmore had seen Lucas come running down the street, dodging through the slow-moving cars and around the dark-coated knots of restaurant-hopping yuppies. She had heard him shout out her name, the sound bouncing around the brick and cobblestone till it acquired a metallic twang. And at the last minute, as the ferry's second and final blast sounded, she'd had to stop herself from getting off the boat and running to meet him.

But she *had* stopped herself.

She didn't want to listen to his pleading and apologies. There would be no forgiveness for what he had done.

She had wanted to hide before he could see her, but she'd felt rooted to her spot at the stern. She looked down at him from high above as he slammed his hand in frustration against the railing while the ferry pulled away, putting inches, then feet, then impassable yards of inky water between them.

Only when he looked up, brushing his lank blond hair back with a painfully familiar gesture, only when his dark eyes met hers, did she at last turn away.

Zoey waited until the ferry was well out into the harbor before looking again. From here, on the unlit deck, half-invisible under an obscured moon, she knew Lucas could no longer see her. But she could see him, a forlorn figure almost alone on the bright landing, small against the backdrop of Weymouth's aged brick waterfront buildings, even smaller against the looming backdrop of modern office high-rises behind them.

He hadn't left to go back to the party. But at any moment he would. Claire was still at the party, and he would surely go running back to her.

Zoey tried to suppress the images that leapt to the front of her mind. She'd always had far too good an imagination. Now it supplied her with all the pictures she didn't need to see: lurid shots of Lucas with Claire, sprawled across the leather seats of Claire's father's Mercedes. Her imagination even supplied the dialogue: *"Claire, you're so wonderful. So unlike Zoey. So much sexier. So much more adult."*

Although, of course, he probably hadn't *said* any of those things. He would have been too busy for conversation. They both would have been far too busy to talk, but oh, they would have thought a few things. The two of them, thinking about the people they were cheating on. Claire cold-bloodedly unconcerned for Jake. And Lucas . . . Lucas probably just thanking his lucky stars that he didn't have to wait around for Zoey to decide whether she was ready. Why wait for Zoey when he could have Claire right now?

At last, with the ferry well out into the bay, she could no longer see him at all. Now she faced the darkness ahead. Chatham Island wasn't yet visible except for the faint green light at the end of the breakwater and the white sweep from the lighthouse at the northernmost tip of the island.

She slumped back onto a cold steel bench and hung her head. Her blond hair streamed back, lifted by the wet, chill breeze. "Lucas," she whispered. But she didn't cry. She'd cried herself dry over the breakup of her parents' marriage. She had no more tears left.

Lucas had cheated on her, just as her mother had cheated on her father. And the result would be the same: it was impossible for any relationship to survive this kind of blow. She would never be able to trust Lucas again.

Nearby on deck, huddling together for warmth, a family. Father, mother, and seven- or eight-year-old son. They weren't Chatham Islanders or she'd have recognized them. They must be going on to Allworthy or Penobscot Island. They'd been shopping on the mainland and carried net stretch bags, like all islanders. The little boy's bag held a costume, the mask visible in its cellophane-windowed box. An X-Man, or something like that.

Halloween was coming up, two weeks away. A depressing thought, not because of Halloween itself, but because Thanksgiving and Christmas followed fast on its heels. The first Thanksgiving without her father at home. And what would have been her first Thanksgiving with Lucas.

Again the images flooded her brain, trailing disgust and jealousy and even, strangely, a sense of guilt in their wake. They mingled inextricably with the images of her mother on that terrible day when Zoey had come home early. Too early and seen what she should never have seen.

Without even intending to, Zoey went back to the railing and gazed at the far-distant landing, now just a bright dot, lost in the lights of the city. Perhaps Lucas was still standing there, realizing what he had lost.

Perhaps he was already back at the party with Claire.

The distant, dwindling light grew blurry. And Zoey realized that she hadn't yet cried out all her tears.

Lucas stood on the pier in an agony of frustration, watching the ferry disappear into the darkness. It was the last ferry of the night. They had all planned on going back home from the party on the water taxi, splitting the forty-dollar cost between the eight of them. He dug his hand in the pocket of his jeans and looked at what he drew out. Nine dollars and two quarters. Not enough.

And what could he say to Zoey anyway? Even if he had been able to explain, just what was he supposed to say? "No, I didn't *sleep* with Claire, we just made out"? That was a lesser offense, certainly, but still not something that would make Zoey rush into his arms, full of forgiveness.

And the truth was he *had* tried to get Claire to sleep with him. He had tried; there was no denying it. At the time he'd thought Zoey was getting back together with Jake. He'd thought he had some justification. But none of that was going to convince Zoey.

No, Lucas realized bitterly. He had been a jerk, and now he was paying for it. Paying with a hurt that was physical in its intensity. *His* fault. Claire was to blame, too, but the real fault was his. No big surprise, that. He had a talent for screwing up.

"So you're my brother," Lara McAvoy said to Benjamin. She squirted ketchup over her plate of fries and ate a long one in two bites. She was pretty, Nina decided, although you almost couldn't tell under the overdone makeup and white-trash hairdo.

Her boyfriend, Keith, sat back in the diner booth. Nina noticed that he looked less handsome under the harsh fluorescent overheads than he had seemed in the dim light of the party. Although he still had excellent rock-star hair.

Benjamin sat beside Nina, across the table from the other two. The fingers of his right hand rested where he could maintain contact with his coffee cup. That way he wouldn't have to feel around for it. He was aiming his opaque black shades in the direction of Lara's voice, giving his usual uncanny impression of being sighted, although of course he saw nothing at all, not even Lara's bold, curious stare.

"Yeah, I'm afraid so," Benjamin said. "I didn't intend to just spring it on you, but things were getting a little out of control . . ."

Nina stole a glance at Keith: the *thing* that had gotten out of control. But there was no acknowledgment. He just watched from beneath half-closed lids.

"And you say I have a half sister, too, huh?"

Benjamin nodded. "Her name is Zoey."

"Well." Lara ate a fry.

Benjamin sipped his coffee. "Yeah."

"I knew I supposedly had a natural father out there somewhere in the world," Lara said. She laughed derisively. "I mean, I knew I wasn't related to that slug my mom married."

She certainly seemed to be taking it well, Nina thought with mild surprise. If Nina had suddenly had some guy pop up and go, "Hey, guess what, I'm your half brother," she was sure she'd have reacted with something more emotional than french fry eating.

"Where does he live?" Lara asked.

"We all live in North Harbor," Benjamin said.

"North Harbor? Where's that?"

"You know, Chatham Island," Benjamin said.

Lara nodded. "Oh, right. That's one of those little islands out in the bay. I haven't lived around here all that long. I used to live down in Kittery until I moved out to get my own place."

"*Our* own place," Keith interjected sullenly, his first contribution to the conversation.

"Is it cool living on an island?" Lara asked. "I mean, do you guys party a lot out there?"

Nina stifled a sarcastic response. This was Benjamin's

10

half sister, after all. They shared the same father. And for that matter, so did Zoey, and Zoey was her best friend. This Lara girl might *look* like a bimbo and *sound* like an airhead, but surely, if she was related to Zoey and Benjamin she had to have some good qualities.

"I like the island," Benjamin said. "Um, so. What do you do?"

"You mean, like, for work?"

"Or school, or whatever," Benjamin said.

Lara shrugged. "I wait tables. I also do temp work sometimes."

Benjamin smiled. "See, it must be a family trait. My folks . . . which is to say, *your* folks, too, to some extent . . ." He took a deep breath. "Anyway, we own a restaurant on the island."

Keith perked up slightly at this. "Like, a good restaurant?"

Probably wants to know if the Passmores are rich, Nina realized. She wondered if Benjamin had thought the same thing. She saw the tiny, ironic smile, quickly suppressed.

"Just a little place for islanders year-round and tourists in the summer." He plastered an innocent smile on his face. "What is it *you* do, Keith?"

"I do whatever," Keith offered.

Uh-huh. Keith *sold* whatever. Whether he also *did* it was an open question, but Nina and Benjamin had followed them around long enough earlier that evening to be sure that Keith, at least, was in the business of selling drugs.

"Anyone mind if I don't smoke?" Nina asked. She retrieved her pack of Lucky Strikes from the bottom of her purse, shook one out, and stuck it unlit in the corner of her darkly lipsticked mouth.

Lara stared at her for a moment, then returned her

11

attention to Benjamin. "So, like, you're blind, huh? You can't see anything?"

"All I can see are reruns of *Full House*," Benjamin said, straight-faced. "It's a weird kind of thing; totally baffles the doctors."

Nina laughed out loud, then stifled herself when it became clear that neither of the other two had gotten the joke.

"So, what am I supposed to say?" Lara asked.

"What do you mean?"

"I mean, like okay, so you're my half brother, right? So, what does that mean?"

"I don't know that it means anything, Lara, except that now you know you have a half brother and half sister and a biological father." He shrugged. "Maybe if you need an organ donation someday . . ."

Lara thought about this for a while as she consumed a few more fries. "You're not just making this up, are you?" she asked finally. She gave Benjamin a strange, sideways look.

"Why would I make it up?"

She shrugged. "Sometimes people tell me things and I don't know if they're real or not."

Nina noticed Keith grinning wryly and chuckling to himself.

"Well, I'll tell you what, Lara," Benjamin said patiently. "No one wants to rush anything or force anything, all right? So how about if I give you my number at home. You think about what you want to do, and if you want to, you can call me, okay?"

Nina fumbled again in her purse and produced a pen. She wrote Benjamin's phone number down on a paper napkin and handed it to Lara. Keith reached aggressively and took it, leaving Lara's hand poised in midair. She shrugged and ate another fry.

"We have to go," Keith said. He looked at Benjamin,

then at Nina. "She'll call you if she wants anything."

Lara stood up and turned her sidelong, skeptical gaze on Benjamin. The look was lost on Benjamin, of course, who kept his shades pointed at the spot where she had been. "Is this all true?"

"All true," Benjamin said.

"Because I heard maybe you just made it up."

"Where did you hear that?" Benjamin asked reasonably.

For some reason Keith found the question funny. He laughed harshly and shook his head in merriment.

"I hear things about people," Lara confided.

"Oh, yeah," Keith agreed sarcastically. "You'd be amazed what Lara hears."

Two

"It's never some little skinny guy who you end up having to carry," Christopher complained. "No, no, it has to be some behemoth."

"Behemoth?" Aisha asked.

"Yeah, behemoth. It's a good word. It means great big dumb white boy who drinks too damned much."

Jake McRoyan was far too drunk to walk unaided. He had consumed a large volume of beer and a smaller, but still dangerous volume of tequila. Aisha had found him collapsed in a corner in one of the bedrooms at the party. He'd been moaning something about Claire being a bitch, which wasn't especially surprising. Jake and Claire had a strange, self-destructive relationship, it seemed to Aisha. Not at all like the mature, rational relationship she herself had with Christopher.

She'd gone to Claire to ask for help in getting Jake to move, but Claire had been coldly indifferent. That *was* a surprise. Claire had stood by Jake in the past when his drinking had gotten out of control. Maybe she'd reached the end of her patience. Claire wasn't renowned for her patience.

So Aisha had drafted Christopher, and now the two of them were half-leading, half-carrying Jake down to the pier to catch the water taxi home. Jake's knees kept splaying out, collapsing his legs. Then Christopher would grab him under his arms and prop him back up and Aisha would offer encouraging words: "It's only another few feet, Jake, come on."

Jake tripped over his own feet and nearly went flying. Christopher kept him from slamming against a concrete light post, but just barely. "Jeez, this guy is heavy," Christopher complained. "I'll bet he's two twenty-five. Damn big lumpy football player. If a guy's going to be a drunk and make people carry his ass around the streets, he ought to be under two hundred pounds."

At last they reached the pier and sloughed Jake onto a bench, where he promptly rolled off and lay crumpled on the ground, passed out.

"Well, he stays there, as far as I'm concerned," Christopher said. "I can't lift that dude. When it's time, we can drag him on board."

"No argument here," Aisha said. She had little enough pity for drunks, and because she'd had to carry Jake, she was sweaty and her clothes were rumpled and the image of a romantic interlude with Christopher on the trip back to the island seemed pretty unlikely now. "You know, I was kind of disappointed by the party tonight. I mean, I was at Richie's last two birthday parties and both times we had some kind of massive explosion or something. Breakups, fights, hair pulling. It was kind of tame this year."

"Maybe we just missed most of the excitement," Christopher said.

Aisha decided she didn't care if she was sweaty and frowzy. Christopher was too, so they were even. She wrapped her arms around his waist and kissed him. "We didn't miss *all* the excitement. I remember certain exciting moments."

Christopher kissed her deeply and slipped his hands inside her coat.

"Christopher, not out here in public," she chided, although without much conviction. "Someone might see."

"No one around but Jake, and he can't see anything right now," Christopher said.

Aisha closed her eyes and reveled in the pleasure for a moment, but when she opened them again, she noticed someone she'd missed seeing earlier.

"Stop it. There's Lucas," Aisha said, pushing Christopher away. "*Without* Zoey," she added in an undertone. He was halfway down the block, sitting and seemingly staring at a docked sailboat.

"What happened, they fight?"

"I don't know. Everything was fine early on, then suddenly I couldn't find Zoey, and Lucas was wandering around looking very bummed."

"Hey, Lucas!" Christopher shouted. "Come here and stop being lazy. Help me get Jake up off the ground. You been sitting there the whole time watching me drag this overgrown monster all the way down here?"

Lucas shambled over and without a word helped manhandle Jake back onto the bench.

"You know, I'm starting to think our man Jake here may have a little drinking problem," Christopher said.

"He doesn't drink all that often," Aisha said.

"Yeah, but when he does, he gets serious about it. I have the occasional brew myself, but no one has ever had to carry me down the street," Christopher said. He looked at Jake with distaste.

"He had a bad night," Lucas said quietly.

"If you're a drunk, you can always come up with some excuse," Christopher countered. "So what's his problem tonight?"

Lucas looked glum and shook his head. Then they heard the sound of heels on cobblestone. Claire, coming down the street in a chic cream wool coat that contrasted sharply with her long, jet-black hair.

Lucas's expression went even darker than it had been. He muttered a particularly foul curse word, moved off a short distance, and turned his back on all of them.

Aisha and Christopher exchanged a significant look. Lucas and Claire had a long history between them, but Lucas wasn't usually one for being quite so vicious.

"I have a feeling Jake's *problem* just showed up," Christopher said in an undertone.

Claire glanced coolly down at Jake and checked her watch. "It's five till one. Where are Nina and Benjamin?"

"And Zoey," Aisha amended.

"I believe Zoey left early and caught the last ferry," Claire said blandly. "Ah. There they are."

Nina and Benjamin were just coming down the street.

"Where have you two been?" Aisha called out. "You missed the dismal last few hours of the party."

"We've been spying and kicking ass," Nina said happily.

"We met my half sister for the first time," Benjamin announced. He grinned complacently at the silence. "We had a delightful time. First we spied on her and her boyfriend, discovering that her boyfriend sells drugs. Then I was chased and pounded by said boyfriend. Then I got in a lucky kick to his balls. And we rounded off the evening with a long and fairly stupid conversation over french fries."

Aisha looked at Christopher. "Okay, I'm starting to think you're right. We missed most of the excitement."

When they disembarked from the water taxi, the seven of them went their separate ways. Claire, directly toward her home without a word to anyone. Nina followed her, but only after she and Benjamin said good night to each other for several minutes that involved a lot of kissing and false departures followed by more kissing. It got on

17

Aisha's nerves a little because she'd have liked to have a similar long farewell with Christopher but Christopher was busy with Lucas, the two of them trying to get Jake off the boat.

"I'll probably still be awake when you come by later," she whispered to Christopher.

"I'll knock on your window," he said, smiling at the prospect.

"Knock quietly. My mother can hear things that no other human being can hear," Aisha warned.

Christopher and Lucas finally went off, half-dragging, half-carrying Jake and discussing the best way to sneak him into his bedroom without alerting his parents.

Aisha walked with Benjamin through the graveyard quiet of North Harbor, down dark, cobblestoned streets where the darkest alley, even at one thirty in the morning, was safe. Here on these streets Benjamin could get around almost as well as a sighted person, the darkness irrelevant to him as he kept his subconscious count of steps from corner to corner.

She left him at his house, asking him to tell Zoey to call her in the late morning after Aisha got back from church. From the Passmore home it was a long climb up the aptly named Climbing Way to the ridge that overlooked the tiny town. Aisha leaned into it, trying to ignore the complaints of her tired muscles.

Aisha lived in a bed-and-breakfast, a huge, painstakingly decorated old home that in summer rented rooms to tourists. This time of year there were no tourists and big parts of Gray House were empty. The family—her mother and father and little brother, Kalif—lived in a separate area upstairs with its own family room, bathroom, and kitchen. Aisha was the only one whose room was downstairs. It made for a feeling of isolation sometimes, but also of privacy.

To her surprise, as she entered the house on tiptoes,

she saw a light in the guest living room just to the right. She peeked inside and saw her father, wearing a bathrobe and snoring in a wing-back easy chair.

Aisha crept over to him and saw that he had a book open on his lap. An illustrated book on birds.

She shook his shoulder gently. "Wake up, Daddy."

"Huh?" He opened his eyes. "What? Oh. I wasn't sleeping."

"Daddy, don't you think I'm a little old for you to be waiting up for me?"

He gave her a sleepy, disgruntled look. "I wasn't waiting up for you." He lifted the book. "I was reading up on cormorants."

"Sure you were," Aisha said.

"And by the way, the answer is no, you're not too old for me to wait up for you," her father said. "You'll never be that old as long as you're my daughter." He got up, groaning as he straightened his back. Aisha gave him a helpful pull.

"Did you have a good time?" he asked.

"It was okay."

"Good." He started off toward the stairs but stopped at the door. "Oh, someone called for you earlier. Long distance."

"Really?" Aisha was intrigued.

"Yes. First he tried to tell me his name was T-Bone. But when I threatened to hang up, he decided his name was really Jeff Pullings."

"Jeff?" Aisha felt her stomach roll. Jeff was calling her? Now? "Did . . . did he say anything?"

"Yes, he said he had a gig." Her father gave her a knowing look. "That means a job for a musician. Gig."

"Yes, I know."

"Oh. Well, anyway, he said he's opening for Salted Peppers and Queen Lateeth in Boston this weekend and he wondered if you'd like to come down."

19

Aisha took a moment to translate "Salted Peppers" into Salt-n-Pepa. "Queen Lateeth" was easier. Latifah.

Then it hit her. Jeff's rap group was opening for two major acts like that? She'd always thought he was good, but this was *major*. At least, she was pretty sure it was major. She'd never paid all that much attention to music. In the morning she'd ask Nina. Nina would know.

"Thanks, Daddy," she said distractedly.

"Well, good night."

Aisha went to her room. She snapped on the lamp by her bed. The clock showed almost two in the morning. In another hour and a half Christopher would come by in his newly purchased island car, delivering papers. He would tap at her window and they would kiss on the front porch or in the warmth of his car, making up for the good-bye they'd had to pass up at the landing.

Christopher, the great love of her life.

So different from Jeff, the *first* great love of her life.

Three

Lucas and Christopher managed to drag and carry Jake from the landing across the ferry parking area, past the Passmores' restaurant, and along the curve of Town Beach. But they still weren't half the distance to Jake's house.

"Man, I was hoping to get an hour of sleep before I had to get up and go to work," Christopher complained.

"I gotta take a rest," Lucas said. He sloughed Jake's arm off his shoulder and the two of them tumbled Jake over the low concrete retaining wall onto the beach.

"We could just leave him there," Christopher suggested hopefully.

Lucas shook his head. "He's had a bad time of it tonight."

"He's hammered. How bad a time could he be having?"

Lucas slumped down gratefully onto the sand, resting his back against the wall. Christopher sat down wearily just on the other side of Jake.

"Why does this remind me of a scene from *Weekend at Bernie's*?" Christopher asked dryly. "Two of us and a dead guy."

As if to deny that he was dead, Jake began snoring fitfully.

"So. What hit the fan with Jake here?" Christopher asked.

"Claire told him I'd slept with her," Lucas said.

"You slept with Claire?" Christopher demanded, simultaneously shocked and envious.

"No. I told you about it, Christopher. We kind of made out was all."

"Yeah, I remember that."

"So Claire told Jake we'd done *it*. Jake gets upset and proceeds to get roasted. Then he goes off and tells Zoey the big news."

Christopher was absently sifting sand through his fingers. "Why'd he tell Zoey?"

Lucas shrugged. "I don't know for sure. But basically I guess Jake still kind of likes Zoey. Maybe she still likes him, too, I don't know."

"Oh, so it's like he's warning her that you're a dog. He figures when she hears about this, she'll dump you and go running to him?"

Lucas sighed. "I don't know, dude. I'm too tired to figure it all out. Except that for whatever reason, Claire lied to Jake. Maybe she was trying to make him jealous. Maybe she just wanted to make him mad enough to kick my ass."

"Women," Christopher said without elaboration.

"Claire," Lucas said darkly. He dug his hand down into the cold sand. The tide was coming in, lapping closer and closer, inch by inch. But they were well up the beach, beyond the reach of the water.

"Maybe she told Jake figuring he'd be sure to tell Zoey," Christopher suggested. "Maybe she wants to break you and Zoey up."

"I'm sure she has some reason," Lucas agreed, "but with her, who knows? No one understands Claire, except maybe Benjamin." He nudged the unconscious Jake. "This poor dude, man, he's just helpless."

"So what are you going to do about Zoey?" Christopher asked. "Tell her, 'hey, babe, I didn't do it with Claire. I tried like hell but I didn't because she wouldn't let me'?" Christopher laughed cynically.

"I'm glad you're entertained by my life falling apart," Lucas said grimly. "Christopher, do you ever think maybe you're just the world's biggest screwup?"

"No, man," Christopher said. "You shouldn't think that way, either."

Lucas stared out into the darkness for a while. "You know what I have going for me if I lose Zoey?" he said at last.

"No. What?"

"Not a single goddamned thing, Christopher," Lucas said. "Not one single thing."

Christopher had no answer for this. He sighed and looked mightily uncomfortable, and at last Lucas forced a lighter tone.

"So. How about if we drag Jake down to the water? Cold seawater in the face might wake him up enough to stagger home."

Christopher climbed to his feet, brushing sand from his pants. "Worth a try."

"Come on, Jake," Lucas said gently. "Time to hit the cold shower."

Aisha sat in her room, on her still-made bed, with her personal photo album open on her lap. The lamp was on, casting a gentle yellow glow. She wore a long flannel nightgown, light gray with pink flowers. On the wall above her bed was a mounted poster of Einstein. On the opposite wall a poster of Stephen Hawking against the backdrop of his book *A Brief History of Time*. Over her desk were photos of Ronald McNair, the astronaut and physicist killed in the *Challenger* explosion, Colin Powell, and Dr. King.

In the book on her lap was a photograph of Jeff Pullings and her, hugging extravagantly. To Aisha's critical eye, she looked like a toothpick topped with lots of hair. Jeff was a head taller, hair cut in a stylish fade, muscular arms bare in a torn, sleeveless denim jacket that was open in front.

She could remember the day the picture had been taken. Aisha with Jeff and his friends, all on a Saturday hanging out by Faneuil Hall Marketplace. Jeff and three other guys had decided they were going to get serious making music, and armed with a turntable, a small amplifier, a tape player, and a lot of D-cell batteries, they were going to entertain the tourists at Faneuil Hall and, no doubt, be overheard by someone with connections to the music industry.

Aisha had thought at the time that it was a silly plan, but Jeff was three years older, an actual *senior* while Aisha was a lowly freshman, so she kept quiet.

As it turned out they played for a while, picked up nine dollars in donations, and finally got rousted by two good-humored cops. The police informed them that there was a city bureaucracy that had to be dealt with if you wanted to play music in public.

Unlike Jeff, Aisha had the patience to learn more. And three months later Jeff got a regular spot rapping in one of the T stations, Boston's public transportation system. During the week commuters on the system got a few minutes of a string quartet as they waited for trains. But on Saturday and Sunday the spot was turned over to Jeff, now, in honor of the "T," calling himself T-Bone.

That's what he was doing when Aisha and her family left Boston. Now he was opening for Queen Latifah and Salt-n-Pepa. Or Queen Lateeth, as her father said. Jeff had come a long way. He was a success, against all the odds. And now he wanted to see Aisha again.

Aisha went to her closet and after some digging pulled

out her old diary. In those days she had written her private thoughts down on paper, protected only by a tiny brass lock that had long since broken. Now when she felt like writing, she put it in her computer, protected by code words. Only, she seldom wrote anything anymore.

Dear Diary: Got an A plus on the stupid math test today and Mr. Lass naturally made a big deal because it was the only perfect score in the class, which was so embarrassing. That little bitch Breonna (gag, retch) called me a mega dweeb

Aisha smiled ruefully and thumbed forward. Fortunately she'd gotten over being embarrassed that she was good in things like math.

Dear Diary: Guess who asked me out? Jeff PULLINGS!!!! He's a SENIOR!!!! I nearly screamed when he said it. No one EVEN believes it's true.

Dear Diary: Mother is totally MENTAL because I'm going out with Jeff. Like just because he's older he's only after one thing. Duh. Like guys my own age aren't just the same. And being older he's so much more mature, so he's

*not all gross about things. I am so abso-
lutely in LOVE with Jeff. I think
someday he'll be a famous musician and
we'll be married and I'll be a model.
Like David Copperfield and Claudia
Schiffer, only not so dorky.*

*Dear Diary: Jeff just left this minute
and I had to write about it instantly. It
was so magical and amazing. He is so mature and so cool. We French-kissed for a
really long time and I even let him
touch under my bra!!! Scream!!!*

Aisha closed the book. The fourteen-year-old Aisha
seemed like another person. A slightly embarrassing person, gushing over Jeff like that. But there was one more
entry she wanted to read again. She remembered the
date.

*Dear Diary: This was the night. The
night when I absolutely became a
WOMAN and not just a little girl.
That's what Jeff told me, that now I
was his woman, not his little girl. In
case you can't guess, dear diary, we finally*

There was a light tapping sound at her window and Aisha started guiltily. She slammed the diary closed and slid it under her pillow.

She caught her breath for a moment, then drew the curtains back. What she saw was a familiar, though distorted face. A President Clinton mask.

She opened the window. "Hi, Christopher."

"Kin ah have some fries with that?" Christopher asked in a bad Arkansas accent.

"Wait, you're not Christopher," Aisha said, feeling guilty but trying to act normal. "You're so much prettier than he is."

Christopher pulled off the mask. "Very humorous."

"Now, what if I had screamed at the top of my lungs and woken up my father and mother?"

Christopher looked thoughtful. "Hmm. I guess I'd have had to run for it." He wiggled his eyebrows suggestively. "Can I come in?"

"No, you can't. I'll be right out."

Aisha closed the windows and drew the curtains again. She pulled on her galumphy L.L. Bean boots, leaving them unlaced, and her puffy green parka over her flannel nightgown. She hazarded a look at herself in the mirror and had to laugh. If Christopher could love her looking like this, he must really love her. What would Jeff think if he saw her in full Maine regalia, looking like a cross between Minnie Mouse and Frosty the Snowman?

She crept silently down the hall and opened the front door carefully. The air was a cold slap, making her face tingle, immediately finding its way under the hem of her nightgown. Christopher came up with the mask back on.

"Kiss me," he whispered. "I'll make you secretary of state."

"It's freezing out here," Aisha said.

Christopher pulled off the mask again, obviously a little disgruntled that she didn't find it as hysterically funny as he did. He put his arms around her, squeezing air from her parka, and pulled her close.

His first kiss was infinitely gentle.

Jeff had always been playful when he kissed her.

His second kiss was deeper, not aggressive, but yearning. She opened her lips.

She remembered the first time Jeff had ever French-kissed her. She'd been shocked and slightly disgusted. But later, when she'd gotten used to it, she'd found it incredibly exciting.

As she did now with Christopher.

As she had then with Jeff.

Christopher's lips were fuller.

Jeff's thinner. And there had been a rasp of whiskers.

Christopher was taller.

Jeff had been broader.

Christopher trailed kisses down her throat, lowering the zipper of her parka to expose more. "Let's go sit in my car," he said in a low whisper.

They walked across the yard to Christopher's shattered, horrible island car. Aisha glanced back nervously at the house. Fortunately her parents' windows were at the back. Unless they came into the family's private living room, they couldn't see the front yard.

Inside the car it was marginally warmer. The radio was on, playing scratchy, staticky, but unfortunately recognizable music. Salt-n-Pepa. "Whatta Man." Aisha snapped it off.

"You don't like the music?" Christopher said.

"It's not coming in very well," Aisha said.

Christopher smiled self-deprecatingly. "It's not exactly a great sound system. But the sad thing is, it's one of the best parts of this car."

"You think *this* is bad?" Aisha looked around at the interior, the sagging headliner, the fact that there were no backseats, the plastic wrap and duct tape that were the right rear window. "For an island car this is nothing. You still have a windshield."

"Don't be dissin' my ride," Christopher joked. "This is as big a piece of crap as anything on the island."

"No way. You have a muffler."

"Well, I have to since I drive around at night," Christopher said defensively. "But how about the paint job? How about the fact that one headlight points left and the other points almost straight up?"

"Hey, in *our* island car only one door opens. And our radio only gets one station, and that's a country station."

"Oooh. That is good," Christopher admitted.

"But I will say you have an excellent stench of mildew," Aisha allowed. "And I like the way the rear bumper is attached with yellow nylon rope. That's a nice touch."

"I'll show you a nice touch," Christopher said in a low, sexy voice.

"You wish."

There was a loud rapping on the roof of the car that made them both jump.

"Uh-oh," Christopher said. He lowered the window on his side. "Hi, Mrs. Gray."

"Well, hello, Christopher," Aisha's mother said.

"I was, uh, delivering the papers?"

"I see them there on the porch," Mrs. Gray said. "Also, I believe I see my daughter. In your car. At three-thirty in the morning."

"We were just saying good night," Aisha said.

"Then say it," Mrs. Gray said, putting some steel into her voice.

"Good night, Aisha," Christopher said, extending his hand formally.

Aisha shook it. "Good night, Christopher."

She climbed out of the car and started toward the house, followed by her mother's vow that they would be discussing this tomorrow. "Oh yes," Mrs. Gray said. "We will definitely be discussing this."

Aisha

I'll tell you what's scary: snakes.
I mean, I know it's a real common
thing to be afraid of, but still, snakes can
be bad news. You can show me Nightmare
on Elm Street one through seventeen
and I don't care. But don't get me
around snakes. You can't trust an animal
that has no legs. I mean a land animal, of
course. Dolphins have no legs and I'm
sure they're fine, but a thing on land
with no legs is not to be trusted. Snakes,
worms, slugs: I have nothing good to
say about any of them.

The other thing that's always kind of
scared me is insanity. You know? Like
the possibility that one day you'd be
going along fine, minding your own
business, and then, all of a sudden, your
brain just loses it. You start hearing
voices in your head, or seeing things
that aren't there? You start gibbering
like an idiot and talking about
conspiracies? It happens. And it's
usually during the teen years that

insanity starts showing up. That's true. They say it's all the hormones associated with going through puberty, and the fact is that the closest I ever came to going crazy was mostly because of hormone-related things. It was like all my life growing up I'd been this perfectly normal girl. Some might even say boring. I mean, I was still in Girl Scouts when I was fourteen, which tells you I wasn't exactly running with the wild and crazy crowd.

But then, when I was fourteen, I did sort of go crazy. Dangerously, stupidly crazy. Only for a while, but enough to know I didn't want to stay that way.

What made me go crazy? Duh. A guy, of course. What else would it be?

Four

Zoey got up unusually early. It wasn't something she'd planned, but despite having fallen asleep very late the night before, she woke up on her usual school-day schedule.

She woke fully alert and with the feeling that she had to be somewhere. A quick mental check showed that she didn't have anything at all to do this morning. Her friends were unavailable on Sunday mornings. Aisha went to church, and Nina had long since made clear that she would kill anyone who bugged her on a Sunday before noon. Lucas also went to church, so she wouldn't be able to see him till later.

Suddenly she remembered.

She wouldn't be seeing Lucas at all, if she could help it.

She showered and got dressed and put on casual clothes, a pair of gray sweatpants and her red fleece jacket.

She went outside and jogged for several blocks, not through any great desire for exercise but just to burn off the wired, overalert feeling.

She jogged as far as the circle and dropped to a walk as she began to encounter the groups heading on foot toward early mass. The island's only church had to handle both Catholics and Protestants. Catholics got the earlier hours.

Zoey told herself she was surprised to see people already filing by on their way to the church. She told herself she was *worried* about the possibility that she might accidentally run into Lucas and his mother on their way to the services. And when she scanned the faces in the cluster of worshipers and didn't see Lucas's, she told herself she was relieved.

She walked on through the circle, feeling disgruntled and confused. She couldn't think of a good reason why she had come out this early, and now she couldn't think of anything to do. Maybe she should brave Nina's wrath and wake her up. There was no good reason why Nina had to sleep until noon. Or even eight.

Claire poured coffee into her covered mug and walked back upstairs from the kitchen, past Nina's second-floor room, to her own third-floor bedroom. She climbed up the ladder set in one wall of her bedroom. It led to a rectangular hatch in the ceiling. From long practice she had learned to hook one arm around the ladder, using that hand to hold her coffee mug and push the hatch open with her free hand.

She climbed up through the hole and out onto the widow's walk, a square platform atop the house with low railings all around and towering brick chimneys at each end.

It was her favorite place in the world.

Up here the breeze almost always blew. The view encompassed all the northern end of Chatham Island, all of the harbor that gave the tiny brick and shingle and cobblestone village of North Harbor its name.

To the north was the black-and-white-striped lighthouse on its tiny rocky islet. To the west the fishing boats rocked at anchor or were tied up alongside the pier. The ferry was just pulling in, appearing slowly and mysteriously from a fog bank like some magician's trick.

Weymouth and the whole mainland were invisible behind the fog. To the south the piney ridge rose from the edge of the village and Claire could make out a glimpse of Gray House, Aisha's home, through the trees.

The breeze wasn't moving the fog, not yet. And there would be little sun to burn it off. Overcast blanketed the entire area, turning the small visible circle of the Atlantic the color of lead.

She looked down at the street below, at Lighthouse Road, which separated the row of old restored captains' homes like hers from the jagged rocks and tumbled granite boulders of the north shore.

Claire saw Zoey at the same instant that Zoey's eyes, looking up, met hers.

Claire sighed. Way too early for this, but it had to be done. It was the necessary last step in the process.

She made a slight wave. Then she held out her hand, making a sign for Zoey to wait. As she turned to descend the ladder it occurred to her that Zoey might not want to wait. Presumably Claire wasn't her favorite person in the world right now.

But no, of course Zoey would wait. Zoey would be hoping against hope that Claire would somehow tell her something to make everything all right.

Oddly enough, Claire realized, that's just exactly what she *was* going to do.

Jake woke to pounding on his bedroom door. The first thing he was aware of was a huge, all-encompassing pain in his head. It throbbed monstrously as he turned his head on his pillow.

With the pain came a terrible thirst. His mouth felt as if it had been stuffed full of cotton balls. He opened his eyes and almost cried out from the pain. Eyes swollen. Stomach sick and sour. Muscles cramped and bunched.

"Jake, get up now. You have to get ready for church."

His mother's voice through his door, seeming impossibly loud.

"Okay," he croaked.

"Are you awake?"

He had to fight down the urge to throw up. "Yes," he said tersely.

"Don't be late," his mother chirped in her relentlessly cheerful way.

He sat up and rolled his legs over the side of the bed. He was still wearing pants, though no shirt. At once he knew he would throw up. He jumped up and raced for his bathroom, almost crying from the pain in his head. He slipped and fell to his knees on the tile floor, clutching the toilet bowl with both arms, and heaved.

When he was done, he rolled onto his back on the tile. He was crying now but too dehydrated to form tears, just racking sobs of misery and pain.

At last he forced himself up and stripped off his pants. Damp sand was in the pockets and down his crotch. He staggered into the shower. He swallowed from the jet, gulping and gulping, then vomited it all back up again.

At last with at least some water working its way back through his system and three Advil, he made his way back to his bedroom, still throbbing with one large head-to-toe pain.

He looked around, befuddled. Obviously he had gotten drunk the night before. Either that or he had been poisoned. Maybe they were pretty much the same thing. He had some memory of a party. He remembered music. A flash of people dancing. A flash of himself dancing with Zoey. A disturbing half-memory of Claire, in shadow, her eyes glittering, as dangerous as a snake's.

Then he remembered it all and wished he could have another drink.

*   *   *

Zoey met Claire in the Geigers' front yard. Claire was still carrying her mug of coffee and looking effortlessly elegant, as always. Zoey was acutely aware of her own relative frumpiness in sweatpants and the fleece jacket.

"Out jogging?" Claire asked pleasantly.

"Just walking. I woke up early and couldn't get back to sleep." Zoey waited for some sign of guilt on Claire's face, but there was nothing.

"Mmm. I wanted to see the fog," Claire said. "It's unusually dense. You can feel the moisture. You know, fog is really just a very low cloud. Warmer air moving in across the cold surface of the water and you get condensation that—"

"Claire, I don't want to talk to you about weather," Zoey snapped, surprising herself. Claire's eyebrows shot up.

"Sorry," Claire said.

"I just want you to know that I think you're a bitch," Zoey said. "I mean, a *real* backstabbing bitch."

Claire colored slightly and stared with hard eyes. "What's your problem?"

"What do you mean, 'what's my problem'?"

"I mean, what's your problem," Claire repeated. "I thought we were having a friendly little chat here, and suddenly you go off." She waved her mug slightly for emphasis.

Zoey faltered. If Claire was just putting on an innocent act, it was a good one. "What do you think I'm going to do, Claire, just act like you and Lucas are no big deal?"

"What?"

"You and Lucas, Claire. You and Lucas."

"What about me and Lucas?" Now she sounded genuinely annoyed.

Zoey peered closely at her. Claire's big, almond-shaped dark eyes showed no evidence of guilt or even worry. "Jake told me all about it," Zoey said, but with less certainty.

"Jake? Now Jake's involved? Zoey, what the hell are you trying to say?"

"Jake told me at the party last night that you slept with Lucas," Zoey blurted.

Claire's rare, cool smile formed slowly. "Jake told you I slept with Lucas. Jake, who hates Lucas for taking you away from him; Jake, who still carries a major torch for you; Jake, who was so drunk he had to be carried home; *that* Jake told you I slept with Lucas."

"That's what he said," Zoey replied as staunchly as she could manage.

Claire sipped her coffee and gave Zoey a disappointed look. "I told Jake that Lucas and I went for a drive a few days ago. I was mad at Jake because I saw you and him hugging each other like you were back together. Lucas saw the same scene. That and other things made us both suspicious that you and Jake were thinking of getting back together. So we went for a drive to discuss it. That's what I told Jake."

Zoey tried to think of something to say, but now she was thoroughly confused. If what Claire was saying was true, then . . . then it had been Lucas who thought *she* was being unfaithful. And it was Lucas who had been wronged. And Jake was the bad guy, not Claire *or* Lucas. "Nothing happened between you and Lucas?"

"I did not have sex with Lucas," Claire said sharply. Then she batted her eyes in a parody of coquettishness. "Although he is cute, isn't he?"

"Oh, no," Zoey said, ignoring Claire's attempt to get a rise out of her.

"I can't believe Jake would tell you a story like that," Claire said. "I suppose it was a clumsy attempt to break you and Lucas up."

"But why would he want that?" Zoey asked.

38

"I told you," Claire said with just a hint of bitterness. "I think he's still in love with you. And"—she shrugged—"we're basically finished as a couple, so, frankly, you're welcome to him."

Lucas had gone to confession the day before, early Saturday morning. He had confessed to using bad language, to lying by omission, and to his normal array of sins associated with the vice of lust. The priest had given him the usual penances, seemingly unshocked by the fact that a teenage boy had lust in his heart.

He took Holy Communion with his mother. She was the main reason he attended mass. His father no longer did, and his mother seemed to appreciate or even need her son's company. He had even, somewhat absurdly, prayed for Zoey to come back to him. But he wasn't generally a big believer in prayer, since he'd spent the first year at Youth Authority praying they'd let him out early and that hadn't exactly worked. Neither had those last-minute prayers when he realized he was facing a pop quiz on some subject he hadn't studied. God had never stepped in and decided to give him a free A. Evidently, what with having to run the entire universe, God had better things to do with his time.

The fog that earlier had drifted across the circle was beginning to lift now as he and his mother stepped out of the church. Departing Catholics mingled cordially with the Protestants who were waiting around preparing to go in.

Lucas saw Jake and his mother standing some distance away. Jake was sitting on a bench, his head hanging practically down to his knees. Lucas grinned with the good-natured sadism sober people often feel toward drinkers. Jake was a classic, textbook picture of a guy with a brutal hangover.

He made his way down the steps as his mother was

peeled off into a discussion having to do with potluck dinners and the need to avoid having duplicate bowls of Jell-O salad. He waved good-bye to her and headed around to the right. He wanted to check out the beach, see if there was any hope of surf. He had a lot to think through, and surfing always helped.

Just as he cleared the crowd, though, he came face-to-face with Zoey.

He stopped dead in his tracks. She was dressed sloppily, for her, but looked painfully beautiful to his eyes.

He tried to find something to say, but where should he start? What should he say? *Hi, Zoey, look, I didn't have sex with Claire, we just made out?*

Zoey came closer, and to Lucas's utter amazement, she put her arms around him, tilted back her head, closed her blue eyes, and drew his face down to her. She kissed him in a way that sent something very much like an electric shock through his system and immediately added to the list of sins he would have to confess next week.

"What?" he said when she drew back at last. "I mean—"

"I have to go see my dad now because I told him I would," Zoey said, "but if we could get together this evening, I would really like a chance to apologize to you."

"Apologize?"

"Claire told me what Jake said was a lie," Zoey said. "I am desperately sorry I suspected you, Lucas. And later I would like to show you just how sorry I am."

She kissed him again, despite the dirty looks of various parishioners, both Catholic and Protestant. Then she took off, leaving Lucas feeling foolish and giddy and aware that he was smiling stupidly and not caring.

The question was: Now that he had the prayer thing working, would it also work on tests?

Five

Claire sat at her computer and typed:

```
C:\ CD AOL\ DOSCIM

C:\ CD AOL\ CIM

WAITING . . .
```

The black screen resolved itself into a field of blue and gray. Enter.

"I'm going to have to upgrade to Windows," she muttered to herself.

She pulled down the bar menu, down-arrowed to CB Simulator, and hit Enter. She typed in her own handle: W-E-A-T-H-E-R-G-I-R-L. Down arrow to General Band, Enter. Arrow to channel 17, Teen Only, Enter. The screen filled with a slow scroll of white words on a black background.

[17] TEEN ONLY

Spanky	AAAAARRRRGGGGHHHH
\<DooMeeeNow\>	never thought that. always said STP sucked.
!WhattaMAN!	spanky get a grip dude
Spanky	EEEEYYYYAAAA!!!!!!!
:)martha	hi everyone
COBAIN	you used to love STP don't lie doo-meee. hi martha.
Spanky	hi martha. i have to scream some more. NNNNOOOO!!! AAAAIIII-YYYEEEE!!!
:)martha	forget your prozac again spanky?

Claire read along for a while, seeing nothing that interested her. Then she accessed the ''who's here'' file and scanned down the list of names. Her heart beat a little faster when she saw the handle ''Flyer''. So he was there, just not saying anything. Was he there hoping she would show up?

She pulled down the Talk option and punched in Flyer's name. A private box opened up on the screen. This conversation would be just between the two of them. No one else could monitor it in any way.

Weathergirl

Hi, Flyer. I was wondering if you'd be here.

Flyer

WG, I was hoping you'd show up. I'm not usually on the system on Sunday afternoon.

42

Weathergirl

Me neither, but I had nothing else to do.

Flyer

Last I heard you were going to a party. How did it go?

Weathergirl

Not great.

Flyer

Problems?

Flyer

Still there, WG?

Weathergirl

I was trying to decide if I should tell you. I did something fairly rotten. I manipulated some things so it looked like . . . well, the details are too complicated to go into. But basically I used some people to get back at my boyfriend. Ex-boyfriend, I guess.

Flyer

Back at him for what?

Flyer

Hello, hello. Still with me, WG?

Weathergirl

It sounds too pathetic.

Flyer

Don't have to worry about being embarrassed with me, WG. I'm just a guy you've never seen, who's never seen you. You won't have to face me at school tomorrow.

Weathergirl

OK. He didn't love me.

Flyer

Oh.

Weathergirl

He was still in love with his old girlfriend.

Flyer

That must have hurt.

Weathergirl

I don't get hurt, Flyer.

Flyer

Everyone gets hurt.

Weathergirl

And now he's the one who's hurt. His former girlfriend now thinks he's a liar.

Flyer

But that doesn't change the fact that he doesn't love you.

Weathergirl

No, it doesn't. Apparently I'm not the type of person that guys fall in love with.

Flyer

I doubt that. You're smart and witty. You have goals and ideas. What's not to love?

Weathergirl

Manipulative, self-centered.

Flyer

And honest about yourself. But I don't know if I should be sad or glad about your boyfriend. Maybe he just wasn't capable of appreciating you. Maybe he just looked at what's superficial. Girls are that way with me, usually. I keep telling them that deep down inside I'm sweet and nice and really interesting.

Weathergirl

If I told people I was sweet, they'd just fall down laughing.

Flyer

Well, I like you, WG. Or should I say Claire?

Weathergirl

WG. That's safer somehow, Flyer.

Flyer

Yes. Friends unseen, unnamed, but friends anyway. Right, WG?

Weathergirl

Right, Flyer. Friends. Bye for now.

Flyer

Bye, Weathergirl.

Aisha was on her way into church behind her mother, father, and Kalif when she saw Zoey putting what looked like very major liplock on Lucas. She grinned and figured whatever argument they were having, they'd gotten over it.

After church she thought of stopping by Zoey's house on her way home, but her mother liked to make a big Sunday brunch after church, which was always great. What was not so great was that her mother was clearly waiting for the right moment to talk to her about what had happened the night before.

She would find a time when Aisha's father wasn't around. Because as Aisha knew perfectly well, her mother wanted to bring up matters that her father knew nothing about.

The opportunity came as they headed toward the family's island car, parked across the circle.

"I think I'll walk home," Mrs. Gray told her husband.

"Up that hill?" Mr. Gray asked skeptically. "In Sunday shoes?"

"It will firm up my butt."

Mr. Gray grinned wolfishly and started to say something, then caught himself. "We'll meet you there. I'll start cutting the fruit."

Mrs. Gray shot Aisha an unmistakable look.

"I'll walk with Mom," Aisha said grimly. She watched her father and brother drive off, feeling like the one last refugee who couldn't get on the flight to freedom.

"About last night," Mrs. Gray began without preliminary as they set off.

"Uh-huh."

"You know I think the world of Christopher."

"But?"

"But I don't approve of you sneaking out of the house after dark to have an assignation," her mother said. She waved to a friend down the street.

"I wasn't sneaking, Mother, and I'm not even sure I know what an assignation is."

"Well, an approximate definition would be 'meeting a boy in his car at nearly four in the morning.' When your mother thinks you're sleeping safe in your bed."

"Oh," Aisha said.

Her mother took her arm and stopped her at the corner of South Street. "Have you had sex with Christopher?"

"Mother, of course not!"

Her mother's face relaxed. They started climbing the hill. It was slow going in heels. Very slow going. Aisha would have just taken off her shoes, but the ground was very cold and very damp. Barely above freezing.

"I just don't want another situation like with Jeff," her mother said. From something in her tone of voice it was clear to Aisha that her mother knew about Jeff's call.

47

"Speaking of Jeff, he called," Aisha said. *Ha. You probably thought I wouldn't tell you.*

"Oh, did he? And what did he want?"

Now who's b.s.'ing who? Aisha thought. She wisely didn't say it out loud. "I guess his group is doing pretty well. They're opening for Salt-n-Pepa and Queen Latifah. They're playing on Halloween in Boston."

Mrs. Gray nodded, as if confirming that of course this was just what her husband had reported to her. "I have to admit, I'm surprised. I never expected much from that boy."

"I always told you he was talented," Aisha said defensively.

For a while they walked on in silence. Then her mother said, "So?"

"So what?"

"So are you going to ask me whether you can go down to Boston and hear him?"

Aisha shrugged. "I figured you'd say no."

"You are right about that," Mrs. Gray said firmly.

Silence again as they climbed the steepest part of the hill. The peak of the inn's roof was just coming into view.

"I'm with Christopher now," Aisha said. "I don't have anything going on with Jeff. Besides, he undoubtedly has a new girlfriend. Probably several."

"Maybe at least one will be his own age this time," Mrs. Gray said darkly.

"Mother, I think I would like to see him play, though. I mean, he's an old friend who's having his first big success. He wants to have all his old friends around to see him do well. It would be impolite to say no." Immediately Aisha winced. Wrong choice of words.

"Yes, you always did have a hard time saying *no* to Jeff Pullings, didn't you?"

"You know what I mean," Aisha said.

48

"And you know what *I* mean," her mother shot back.

"It's not like I would be staying with him or anything. I probably wouldn't even get a chance to talk to him. We'd all go down on Friday evening and drive back that same night."

"Who is 'we'?"

Aisha shrugged. "I was going to ask everyone. You know, the usual."

"And Christopher?" her mother asked pointedly.

Panting slightly from the exertion, they had reached the front gate.

"Yes, of course, Christopher too," Aisha said, trying to sound much calmer than she felt. "Why wouldn't I ask Christopher to go with me?"

"Does Christopher know about you and Jeff?"

Aisha looked down. "No one knows about all that. Except you and me. I don't think my friends would even believe it."

For a while they stood silently, remembering. Finally her mother said, "I guess if you went down there with a bunch of your current friends, you might be able to stay out of trouble."

"You mean I can go?"

Her mother nodded slowly. "Yes. It would be wrong of me to go on punishing you for something that happened three years ago."

49

Six

"Hello, is Jeff Pullings there?" In the background a loud, steady drumbeat. The person who had answered the phone was a girl. She asked Aisha to speak louder.

"I'm calling for Jeff Pullings!" Aisha yelled.

"You mean T-Bone?"

Aisha rolled her eyes. "Yes."

"He's busy."

"Tell him it's Aisha Gray."

"Okay," the girl said, telegraphing her reluctance.

Aisha waited with the phone to her ear. Did she really even want to do this? Too late to back out, of course, since she'd given the girl her name. But did she want to accept Jeff's invitation, really? Or—

Suddenly the noise stopped. There was a scuffling sound and someone yelled, "You guys shut the — up; I have a call.

"Eesh? Is that really you?"

"Yes," Aisha said, suddenly breathless. "I'm calling back because my dad said you left a message."

"It's good to hear your voice," he said.

"It's good to hear yours, too," Aisha said. What else could she say? It wasn't like it was any big deal to say it was good to hear someone's voice.

"How are things in Maine?"

"Oh, you know. Same old stuff. School mostly. How are things in Boston?"

"Lonely," he said.

"Lonely?" the word came out in a quiver.

"I'm all alone here in the big city."

"Yeah, Boston is so much bigger than Chatham Island," Aisha said. She rolled her eyes. Could she have thought of anything dumber to say?

"So, are you going to be able to come down? I'd like you to be there. It's a big deal, babe. Major stuff."

"I know; I couldn't believe it when my dad told me," Aisha said with genuine enthusiasm. "You know what he said? He said you were opening for Queen Lateeth."

Jeff laughed at that. "It's a benefit for AIDS. Salt-n-Pepa and Latifah together, and they wanted to include a local act. Which is me."

"I'm really happy for you."

"Yeah, me too. They actually *pay*. Not a lot, but it's a start. Plus, I get picked up in a limo, which beats catching the yellow line." Then, in a more serious voice, "By the way, Aisha, does your father know about me and you? He sounded like he wasn't too happy I was calling."

"No. He can never remember my friends' names," Aisha said. "And my mom never told him the other stuff. He gets upset by things like that."

"Yeah," Jeff said.

For a moment silence fell between them. Aisha felt the edge of sadness. Memories hovered at the boundaries of conscious awareness, threatening to take shape. Memories very good, and very bad.

"Anyway," she said at last.

"Anyway," he repeated.

"So, I'll definitely try to come," Aisha said.

"Don't say you'll *try*," Jeff said. "Say you'll be there."

"Can I bring some friends?"

"Hey, the more people come, the better I like it," he

said. "How many tickets you want? Not too many, I hope. We are just the opening act. Most of the freebies go to Cheryl, Sandy, De De, Latifah. If you have too many friends, they'll have to be on their own."

"Cheryl, Sandy, and De De, huh?" Aisha laughed. "Now you're on a first-name basis with them?"

Jeff echoed her laughter. "Oh, I'm down with all the big stars now."

"Uh-huh."

"Okay, maybe we haven't actually met, and they have no idea who I am exactly, but I have talked to some guy who works for them. And he said, 'Look, kid, just make sure you do a quick set, no encore, and get your equipment the hell off the stage.' So you can see I have a huge amount of respect in the industry."

"Yeah, but it's a major, major step up from playing in the T station."

"Definitely."

"I'm proud of you, Jeff," Aisha said sincerely.

"Will you be there?"

"I'll be there."

"And your friends?"

"Whoever wants to come, I guess," Aisha said.

"Are these just friend friends? Or is there a *friend*?"

Aisha gulped. "Just friends," she said automatically.

"That's what I wanted to hear," Jeff said, sounding relieved. "I better go. Everyone's standing around here giving me the eye, like what am I doing when we should be rehearsing. See you there, babe."

"Wait, Jeff—" But the line had gone dead. Before Aisha could tell him that . . . that what? That one of those friends was named Christopher and yes, he was much more than just a friend?

Yes, that's what she was getting ready to tell Jeff. Only there hadn't been time.

* * *

Nina lay on her back on the rug with two pillows behind her head. Her legs were propped on the side of Benjamin's bed. Benjamin sat on the bed, leaning back against the wall. Nina held a large paperback book over her head and read aloud: *"Round she went: the squared main and mizen yards lay parallel with the wind, the topsails shaking. Farther, farther; and now the wind was abaft her beam, and by rights her sternway should have stopped; but it did not; she was still traveling with remarkable speed in the opposite direction. He filled the topsails, gave her weather helm, and—* Good grief, Benjamin, this book is full of this kind of sailing stuff!" Nina cried. *"Abaft her beam?* What does that even mean?"

"Abaft her beam," Benjamin said placidly.

"Do I have to read all these dumb sailing parts? I mean, what's with this writer anyway? The romantic parts he just skims over, but he has to give you absolutely every single detail of what sail you should use to sail a boat that doesn't even exist anymore!"

"A *frigate*, not a boat, which you would know if you were paying attention to what you're reading," Benjamin pointed out.

"This is like 'boy' book to the maximum amount possible. Sailboats and cannons and all the women back on shore while the guys go off and have fun."

"Well, I *am* a boy," Benjamin said reasonably. "Girls read books about relationships and female things like feelings and emotions, while boys read books about cool stuff involving ships and cannons."

Nina sat up. "I can't believe you'd say anything so sexist. Girls don't just care about relationships. We like other stuff, too. You sexist hound. You *male*, you."

"Really?" Benjamin looked thoughtful. "I hadn't realized that." He grinned. "Then I guess you'll enjoy reading me the rest of the chapter."

"You think you're so cute, don't you?" Nina demanded. And he was. He was so cute. Even when he was smiling that annoying, superior smile, he was so cute. It was funny, because when she'd first started going out with Benjamin, she'd thought the cool thing about a boyfriend who couldn't see would be that she could dress however she wanted, not wear makeup and so on.

But the most excellent thing about Benjamin was that she could look at *him* as long as she wanted, anytime she wanted, without him knowing it. She enjoyed watching his mouth when he smiled his ironic smile; and often, lying around his house, he'd wear a pair of old sweatpants that had been shrunk in the wash to the point where they would sometimes be as tight as a second layer of skin, and that wasn't bad to look at, either.

"Are you going to go on reading, or are you daydreaming?" Benjamin asked.

"Daydreaming," Nina admitted.

"About what?"

"Let's get back to reading," she said. She finished reading the rest of the chapter, outrageously overemphasizing every mention of sails, and looking up each time to the reward of his smile.

"That's the chapter," Nina announced, closing the book. "Now it's my turn."

"Your turn for what?" Benjamin asked suspiciously.

Nina fumbled in her purse and produced a CD. "I just bought this excellent CD . . ."

"Oh, no," Benjamin groaned.

"And since your stereo is so much better than mine . . ." Nina went on.

"Just tell me it's not rap, or Red Hot Chili Peppers or anything."

"It's Redd Kross. Even *you* will like it."

"Want to bet?" he grumbled.

Nina sat down on the bed beside him. She kissed his

lips, feeling amazingly bold, even after all the many times she'd kissed him.

"Okay," he said. "You can play it, but only if you put on rubber gloves and a surgical mask before touching the holy stereo. Also, no touching any buttons except play, *including* the volume. It's perfect right where it is."

"Absolutely, cross my heart," Nina vowed as she twisted the volume knob up and cranked the bass. Just as she hit play she heard the phone ringing in the kitchen. "You want me to get that?"

"Sure," Benjamin said. "If you don't mind. And bring a soda when you come back."

Nina had reached the kitchen by the time the first blast came from the stereo, rattling the windows and vibrating the floor. Nina grinned happily and caught the phone on the third ring, just before the answering machine could engage.

"Yo, Passmore residence."

"Who is this? Nina?" Aisha's voice.

"Yeah, you got a problem with that?" Nina said, putting on a belligerent voice.

"Jeez, Nina, what are you doing over there, having a party? I can practically hear the music without using the phone."

"Wherever I go, it's a party," Nina said. She searched the pantry shelf distractedly. Low-fat cookies. What was the point? "What's up, Eesh?"

The music suddenly dropped precipitously in volume. "Now you're in trouble!" Benjamin yelled.

"I was calling to see if you guys wanted to go to a concert on Halloween, down in Boston," Aisha said.

"Sure," Nina agreed instantly. "Who's playing?"

"Salt-n-Pepa and Queen Latifah. It's a benefit."

Nina held out the receiver and stared at it. "Excuse me? You say you're Aisha? Aisha Gray? Aisha 'hey, I don't think elevator music is so bad' Gray?" Nina banged the receiver several times on the countertop.

"I listen to music," Aisha said defensively.

"Aisha, you are the living, breathing proof that not all black people have rhythm. You couldn't keep the beat in time with Barney singing the 'I love you, you love me' song. You're worse than Benjamin. At least he really loves music. Not always the *right* music, but music. Whereas you own what, three CDs? And two of them are of that computer-music crap." She carried the receiver over to the refrigerator.

"Are you about done abusing me?" Aisha asked patiently.

"Mmm, I guess so. Hey, toaster strudel! Damn, it's cherry. Who on earth buys cherry toaster strudel? In Pop-Tarts and toaster strudel it's blueberry, maybe raspberry. Not cherry."

"Can we focus here a little? I have this friend whose group is opening for Salt-n-Pepa and Latifah at the Orpheum. I have free tickets. Are you in or out?"

"In, duh. Like I would say no?" Nina said. "Benjamin, too."

"Benjamin? At a rap concert? How are you going to get him there—use handcuffs?"

"Hey, we'll be there," Nina said. "I can't believe you have a friend who's in a band. I thought all you knew were math dweebs and techno-dorks."

"I know some just plain dweebs and dorks, too," Aisha pointed out. "After all, I know *you*."

"If I didn't have toaster strudel to soothe me, that would have hurt," Nina said. "I'll tell Zoey when she comes back, too, okay?"

"Sure. Like I wouldn't ask her? The more people the better. Oh, by the way, since it's on Halloween they're telling people to come in costume."

"Okay, now we're getting somewhere," Nina said. "Costumes, a concert, a trip down to Boston. Life has regained its meaning."

Seven

During his seventeen years of life Lucas Cabral had been tripped up repeatedly by one type of lie or another, and one type of secret or another. The problem was, he had never been tripped up consistently in either one direction or the other. Sometimes he had told lies and it worked out fine. Other times lies had gotten him in trouble. Sometimes keeping secrets had been a good idea, other times not so good. Sometimes, even when he did all the right things, when he was absolutely honest and open, he'd still gotten racked up.

What made it worse was that by some twist of fate he always seemed to be stumbling across other people's secrets. At any given moment he knew something about someone that he wasn't supposed to tell. It wasn't his fault; in fact, he tried hard never, ever to learn anyone's secrets, but it didn't help.

He thought all this through as he stood on the wooden deck behind his house. The deck was a few dozen feet up the side of the ridge, where Climbing Way made its first big loop. The deck was almost directly above the backyard of Zoey's house and gave him a view straight down to her kitchen, breakfast nook, and family room.

When it was dark, as it was now, and when the Passmores had their lights on, as they did now, he could see inside: seldom heads, which were cut off by the angle, but bodies sitting around the table, or, like now, Benjamin searching the refrigerator. It was probably wrong to look, Lucas reflected, but it was fascinating. Benjamin moved his hand slowly over each item, tentative and sensitive, recognizing milk, soda cans, poking into the plastic wrap that covered a bowl.

Zoey came into the room. Lucas could see from her body language that she was watching her brother, torn between helping, which would likely earn a sarcastic rebuke from Benjamin, and staying out of the way.

Benjamin's fingers touched a Rubbermaid container. He pulled it out and opened it triumphantly.

For her part, Zoey grabbed a soda and walked over to the window. Instinctively Lucas stepped back into the shadows. Zoey was peering, neck craned, up toward him. Could she see him? Probably not, as dark as it was. But her face looked questioning. She checked her watch.

Waiting for me to come down, Lucas realized with great satisfaction. From back in the shadows he looked at her face, framed by somewhat disarranged blond hair. There was no part of her face that was unfamiliar to him, yet he wasn't in the least way tired of looking at it. He fell asleep every night recalling that familiar face. True, sometimes there were other things about Zoey, not actually familiar but imagined, that also played a part.

She stepped away from the window and he moved forward. He hopped the deck railing, hanging out over empty space for a moment. Then he dropped to a sitting position, twisted to catch the edge of the deck platform with his fingers, and lowered himself down. With his boots just three feet from the Passmores' lawn he dropped, rolled, and stood up.

He walked around the circumference of the house to the front door and knocked.

The door opened on Benjamin, munching a piece of

fried chicken. "Hey, babe," Benjamin leered. He advanced on Lucas with greasy lips puckered up. "Give me a big wet one."

"Very funny, Benjamin," Lucas said, not at all convinced.

Benjamin grinned. "Oh, it's you, Lucas. Imagine my embarrassment."

"How do you do that?" Lucas demanded, sliding past Benjamin.

"I hear a loud dropping noise in the backyard," Benjamin said. "Soon thereafter there's a loud, *male* knock at the door. Also, Zoey's been all skittish like she's waiting for someone."

"Where is Zoey?" Lucas asked.

"How would I know?" Benjamin cried in sudden anguish. "She could be anywhere! I can't see her! She could be right . . . there!" He pointed suddenly at the coatrack.

Lucas rolled his eyes and waited patiently.

Benjamin took another bite of chicken, perfectly calm. "You're no fun, Lucas," he said. "You never fall for anything. Zoey's at the top of the stairs, eavesdropping on us."

"I am not." Zoey's voice floated down the stairs. Followed by her laughter.

Lucas ran up the stairs and caught her up in his arms. He kissed her and at the same time lifted her feet off the floor and carried her toward her bedroom.

They closed the door behind them.

Lucas kissed her again, but then she held him off, giving him a serious look. "I really am sorry I doubted you. It's just that Jake sounded like he was sure, and besides, you know, Claire is . . ."

"What?"

Zoey shrugged. "She is slightly beautiful."

"No, *you* are beautiful."

"And she's kind of sexy, I guess."

"No." Lucas shook his head solemnly. "You're the one who's sexy."

"Anyway, I guess I could see where if she wanted to do it, you'd probably have a hard time saying no."

Now was the time if he was ever going to tell the truth. All he had to say was "look, Zoey, to be honest, while Claire and I did not have sex, we *did* make out. It was meaningless to both of us and it will never happen again."

That's what he should say if he was ever going to tell the truth. But truth hadn't always worked out all that well for him, and this was a case where a small lie of omission was probably the best policy.

Besides, he would be telling the absolute, undiminished truth when he said, "Zoey, I love you with all my heart."

Next confession he would have to remember the sin of lying by omission. And the other, very familiar sin of lust as he kissed Zoey again, and again, and again until at long last, and much later, she once again, gently but firmly, stopped him from committing the next sin.

LUCAS

WHAt Am I AfRAid of? Hmmm. I kind
of don't like small spaces, I
guess. FoRtunAtely when I wAs in
the Youth Authority it wAs All
bARRACKS style, not little
cells. BARRACKS ARe okAy As long As
you don't hAve A feAR of snoring oR of
being knifed in youR sleep.

My otheR big feAR is of myself. I
hAve An AmAzing Ability to scRew
up my life. I got myself thRown in
jAil foR something I didn't even
do; thAt wAs one exAmple. A
fAiRly mAjoR exAmple. And I seem
to be doing my best to mess up my
RelAtionship with Zoey, which is
the most impoRtAnt thing in my
life, foR AnotheR exAmple. So
bAsicAlly if I cAn stop scRewing
up And stAy out of confined
spAces, I'll be fine. But to be
honest, I don't put much fAith in
my Ability to deAl with stuff
successfully.

I guess I AlwAys figuRed I'd

end up a loser of one type or another. When I got back to Chatham Island after jail and everyone made it pretty obvious that they wanted me to go away, I figured, well, that's it, you're marked forever as a loser. But then I was cleared. And more important, I fell in love with Zoey, and for some amazing reason she fell in love with me. I started thinking maybe I'm not such a loser, you know? Maybe in spite of myself things will work out okay.

Except that my relationship with Zoey hangs by a thread, and if she finds out the truth and leaves me for good . . . well, that's what I'm afraid of. To have had something wonderful and perfect and incredible in my life and then to screw it up.

Eight

S	**M**	T	W	T	F	S

On *Monday* Aisha got definite commitments from Christopher, Zoey, and Lucas that they would like to attend the concert in Boston. Claire seemed unenthusiastic about the idea but didn't give a definite no. Jake gave a definite no. It was a curt, almost rude no, like he didn't even want to be talking to Aisha or, for that matter, anyone. He had stuck to himself on the ferry ride over to school that morning.

Benjamin also gave a definite no, but Nina said that he *meant* yes.

S	M	**T**	W	T	F	S

On *Tuesday* Aisha went to the mall after school with Nina and Zoey, supposedly to shop for possible Halloween costumes. But everything she considered seemed either dorky or like she was trying too hard, or not trying hard enough. She ended up buying a new purse that she didn't really like, just because it was on sale, normally seventy-two dollars, marked down to nineteen ninety-five. Zoey bought an earring for Lucas. Nina bought a set of drawing pens and a long black wig and a size 36 double-D bra to be part of a costume whose details she wouldn't reveal.

Nina claimed Benjamin had agreed to attend the concert.

S	M	T	**W**	T	F	S

On *Wednesday* Aisha awoke with memories of a very disturbing dream. In the dream Jeff and Christopher were fighting over her and she was fourteen again. At school that day she aced a calculus test and got a *C* plus on a French quiz. Coming home from school on the ferry, she asked Benjamin if he was coming to the concert, and Benjamin said he would rather be boiled in oil than be trapped in a rap concert. Nina explained that he *meant* yes.

S	M	T	W	T	F	S

On *Thursday* Aisha realized she still hadn't decided what costume to wear, if any. She wanted to look good for Jeff, and at the same time, she didn't. For the first time in talking to Christopher she used the words "old boyfriend" instead of "old friend" in mentioning Jeff. It took an hour and many, many reassurances to convince Christopher that it had all been nothing but a little freshman crush on an older guy who seemed cool. She didn't like lying, but at the same time she couldn't really tell Christopher the whole truth.

Benjamin called to say that no matter what Nina said, he would cut off his legs with a chain saw before he would go to a rap concert.

S	M	T	W	T	F	S

On *Friday* Aisha began to panic. She didn't want to see Jeff again. What was she thinking of? It was insane. She was totally in love with Christopher, and totally committed. And what she'd had with Jeff was history now. Ancient history. What she was feeling was just stupid nostalgia, mostly over a younger, maybe wilder Aisha. An Aisha who no longer existed.

She had to call Jeff and tell him how many tickets she needed. He was out, so she talked to his sister, relieved not to have to deal with Jeff while she was feeling confused. She ordered seven tickets. Herself, Christopher, Zoey, Lucas, Claire, even though she still wasn't sure, Nina, and Benjamin.

That night she had another dream. In this one she remembered the day her mother had taken her out of school and gone with her to the doctor. She woke up in a cold sweat and waited up until Christopher came by with the papers. She made out with him through the window and drove the dream and Jeff from her mind.

Saturday evening Claire logged on to America Online, as she had done every night for two weeks now. And as had happened each night for two weeks, Flyer was there waiting. It had become a ritual between them. It had

65

become the "place" Claire went in the evenings when she was done with homework.

Sometimes they talked for a long time, hours even. Other nights Claire kept it short. Two days earlier she had cut him off to climb up to the widow's walk and watch a wicked squall blow through. But an hour later, when the wind and lightning had rolled off out of sight over the Atlantic, she had gone rushing back to tell him all about it. And he had listened. Not laughing at her fascination, or writing her off as strange for sitting out in the middle of a storm. And she had told him how it felt to be up there, the storm all around her. In telling him she had explained it to herself: the feeling of powerlessness and awe; the sense of clean starts and change.

She typed in "Hello, Flyer."

Flyer

Hi, Weathergirl. Any more storms tonight?

Weathergirl

No. Clear and cold with lots of stars. Beautiful, I suppose, but boring.

Flyer

Same here. It's good weather for flying, though. I took the plane up after school today and did some

There was a knock at the bedroom door. "What?" Claire said in a loud voice.

The door opened and Nina poked her head in. "Hey, Eesh is down in my room. She says are you coming to the concert or not?"

"Didn't she already get me a ticket?"

"What are you doing?" Nina asked, inviting herself in.

Claire quickly punched the Escape key, clearing the screen. "Nothing."

Nina gave her an amused look. "Sitting home on a Saturday night talking to computer dweebs? I can't believe it's come to this, Claire."

"I notice you're home tonight, too," Claire replied. But she had been thrown by Nina's nosiness. She'd told no one about Flyer.

"We're all putting off the usual Saturday night date because we're going to the concert on Halloween," Nina said.

Claire raised an eyebrow. "Benjamin is going, too?"

"Sure. He's excited about it," Nina said. "So, are you in or out?"

Claire sighed. "Look, Nina, Aisha has already ordered me a ticket, right? So I'm in. And if I decide not to go, *you* can have my ticket and sell it to someone at the door."

"Isn't scalping tickets illegal?" Nina asked suspiciously.

"I'm not sure, but you know, Nina, sooner or later you'll end up in jail, so why not get some experience early?"

"Very funny. Tell that to your compu-dorks."

"Go away now, Nina."

Weathergirl

Sorry I bailed, Flyer, but my little sister barged in.

Flyer

And you don't want her to know about me?

Weathergirl

No, I guess not.

Flyer

Why not? I'm just some guy you talk to on the net.

Weathergirl

You're a lot more than that, Flyer.

Flyer

Am I?

Weathergirl

Yes. To me you are. In some ways right now you're the closest friend I have.

Flyer

I am incredibly happy you said that.

Claire took her fingers from the keyboard and stared at her own words there on the screen. Had she just said that? Was it true? God, was her best friend really some guy she only knew via computer? She typed:

Weathergirl

It hadn't occurred to me until just this moment. But I guess it's true. I tell you things I don't tell anyone else. I suppose that makes you a friend.

Flyer

I guess I've felt right from the start that there was something special between us. Maybe it is strange, but I feel like I know you better than I know anyone. I sit here typing in my room and feel closer to you than to anyone.

Weathergirl

I suppose I should sign off now.

Flyer

I haven't upset you, have I?

Weathergirl

No, Flyer. It is strange, though, isn't it?

Flyer

Caring about someone you've never seen face-to-face? Whose voice you've never heard. Yes, it is strange, WG. And yet I do care about you. If it wasn't so improbable, I suppose I might even say that I love you. As much as it's possible to love someone under these circumstances.

Claire stared at the words scrolling up on the screen. Now he was going too far. This was ludicrous. She had never even seen Flyer. She knew his real name was Sean, just as he knew her real name. But what else did she know about him? That he was smart, kind, understanding? Yes. That he always made her feel better about life and especially herself when she spoke to him? Yes. But was that enough?

Weathergirl

I care about you, too, Flyer.

Flyer

That's better. Now you can sign off. You leave me very happy.

Weathergirl

Good night, Sean.

Flyer

Good night, Claire.

"Look, I said he was a *boy*friend," Aisha said. "I admitted he was a boyfriend. You two think I never had a boyfriend in my life before I came here?"

Nina and Zoey exchanged a look.

"Frankly, no, we don't think you ever had a boyfriend before you came here," Zoey said.

They were in Nina's room. An old Breeders CD played on the stereo, at reasonable volume for once. The three of them were sitting cross-legged on Nina's bed around a bag of chips.

"I had a life before you two even knew me," Aisha said.

"You came here when you were fourteen," Nina pointed out. "No one has a life by the time they're fourteen. I'm *six*teen and I just barely have one. Claire's seventeen and look at *her*. She's up there talking to fellow devil worshipers on her computer."

"I'm just saying he was my boyfriend, that's all I'm

saying. It's no big deal, but don't act like I'm making it all up.''

Nina took the unlit cigarette out of her mouth and pointed it at Aisha. ''You were a freshman. And no offense, but I'll bet ten dollars you were a member of the chess club and the honor society. You didn't loosen up at all till you started going with Christopher.''

''For your information,'' Aisha said hotly, ''I was more loosened up *before* I ever moved here. I was in Boston, after all.''

''Oooh, Boston,'' Nina said, cracking herself up.

''Stop picking on Aisha,'' Zoey said mildly.

''I can defend myself,'' Aisha said haughtily. ''I'm just saying that while you two were probably still secretly playing with Barbie dolls, I was going with a senior.''

''Going with,'' Nina echoed in a stage whisper. ''That means she said hello to him in the hallway on her way to class.''

''I could tell you something that would make you take that back,'' Aisha threatened. Instantly she knew she had gone too far. Nina and Zoey were exchanging interested, wary looks.

''She wants to tell us something,'' Nina said.

''It sure sounds that way,'' Zoey agreed.

''Hmm, Aisha has a secret.''

''No fair,'' Zoey said, taking up the bantering tone. ''*We* don't have any secrets.''

''Forget it,'' Aisha muttered.

''Yeah, right,'' Nina said with a derisive laugh.

''Look, it's private, all right?''

''Private having to do with this alleged boyfriend?'' Nina pursued, using her cigarette to stab the air. ''I don't think so.''

Zoey was looking at her thoughtfully. ''Is it something dumb like—''

71

"I slept with him," Aisha blurted suddenly. The second the words were out of her mouth, she wished she could call them back. Zoey and Nina had frozen, mouths open. "Well, you dragged it out of me," she said defensively.

"You mean you *slept* or you had sex?" Zoey asked for clarification.

"We did it," Aisha said. "Okay? Are you happy now?"

Again Nina and Zoey exchanged looks.

Nina said, "I don't know about happy, but you certainly do have our attention, Eesh. Is this for real, or are you yanking us around?"

"Why didn't you ever tell us? I've been your friend for three years!" Zoey said.

Aisha shrugged and looked down at the chips. Telling them the truth was seeming less and less like a good idea. But the secret had begun to preoccupy her, now that she was going to see Jeff again. She'd almost put it out of her mind, it seemed, until his call had reawakened all the old memories.

"Wait a minute, are you doing it with Christopher, too?" Nina asked.

"No," Aisha said. "I don't do that anymore. At least not yet anymore, if you know what I mean."

"Wow," Nina said, awestruck. "So it was like really bad, huh?"

Aisha sighed. "That's not it," she admitted. "That part was nice, mostly."

"You didn't catch something, did you?" Zoey asked intensely. "I mean, it would be okay if you had . . ."

"Okay, look, stop pestering me," Aisha said. "I'll tell you, all right? We did it a few times. And then I missed my period and I was like a week late. So I had to tell my mom."

"Didn't you use anything?" Nina demanded.

"We used condoms except for one time when Jeff didn't have any. He told me one time wouldn't be a problem. You know, like what were the odds that I was going to get pregnant or anything?"

"Wow. So what happened?"

"My mom took me to her gynecologist and I wasn't pregnant or anything, but naturally my mom went off. I mean *way* off. She drove me down to the welfare office and parked outside and was pointing to all these teenage girls with babies going in and yelling is that the way I wanted to end up and so on and on and on."

"Wow," Nina repeated.

"Yeah," Aisha agreed. "Scared the hell out of me, the whole thing. I mean, seriously. I thought I was either going to have to get an abortion or end up living on welfare in some project."

"I can't picture you with a baby," Zoey said. "I mean, you're not stupid, obviously."

"Not stupid?" Nina echoed incredulously. "She's already been accepted to Harvard. As a teacher. Next to you, Zoey, Aisha's the biggest suck-up, goody-goody, get-all-my-homework-done-on-time, study-every-night, wave-your-hand-and-go-ooh-ooh-I-know-the-answer, teacher's pet I know."

"Thanks, Nina," Aisha said dubiously.

"Who would have guessed you were hiding a deep, dark past?" Nina said.

No one, if I'd kept my big mouth shut, Aisha realized. "You both have to swear you'll never, ever tell anyone. I mean, absolutely no one."

"No problem," Nina said.

"Of course not," Zoey said.

"And Nina, when you tell Benjamin, make sure he knows not to tell anyone, too," Aisha added.

Nine

On Halloween, Zoey skipped class for only about the second time in her life. Aisha was anxious to get down to Boston as early as possible and avoid the dreaded Boston rush hour. It was extremely odd for Aisha to want to dump a class, especially her sixth-period calculus, but she was determined, so Zoey decided to go along. Lucas, of course, could be convinced quite easily to dump the afternoon classes.

Benjamin was the holdout. There was plenty of time for him to get through last-period physics and still get down to Boston in time for the concert. No one wanted to argue since Benjamin was at a severe disadvantage in physics, a class that depended too heavily on blackboard equations he couldn't see, and in which he was struggling to maintain a good grade.

Besides, even as he made plans to go, he was still denying he was going at all.

With Benjamin staying till the end, naturally Nina did, too.

Claire, likewise, wanted to wait until the end of the day. She had been quite mysterious about why she was even going along. No one believed she suddenly liked rap, but at the last minute she had accepted the invitation, surprising everyone.

Only Jake had steadfastly refused.

A little after noon, under threatening gray skies, Aisha, Christopher, Zoey, and Lucas piled into the Grays' Ford Taurus and headed south. Their Halloween costumes were in the trunk.

It was three twenty when Claire drove off after them, alone in her father's Mercedes, turning on the wipers to deal with a chilly drizzle. She had no costume, despite Nina's repeated suggestion that she go as Morticia.

It was three thirty-five when Nina and Benjamin followed in the Passmores' van, with Nina driving through puddles and squinting at what had become a driving rain.

At four, Jake drank the three bottles of beer he found in his refrigerator. He no longer worried what his father would say about his beer disappearing. He only worried where and how he could find more.

Ten

Interstate 95 had been a nice, easy drive all the way, despite occasional showers that slowed traffic coming through New Hampshire. Aisha drove the whole way, her mind far from the conversation that floated back and forth between Christopher, Zoey, and Lucas. At first she tried to keep up a regular contribution, but as they passed by Portland, and through New Hampshire, and reached the big "Welcome to Massachusetts" sign, she barely managed the occasional "yeah" or "uh-huh."

She turned up the music on the radio, hoping to discourage further conversation. She didn't want to pay attention. She wanted to remember.

It was her first return to Boston since the family had moved to Maine. She watched the way the interstate grew from two lanes in either direction to three, to four. The number of overpasses multiplied steadily. The speed and aggressiveness of the drivers around her rose sharply.

A closed-in, almost claustrophobic feeling also grew. It was as if walls were growing higher around her, shutting out more of the sky. All the trees were behind her now; only gas stations and restaurants and grim, tall apartment buildings could be seen.

Boston. It reminded her of how small Weymouth really was, and how infinitesimal Chatham Island was. The entire population of Chatham Island could be housed in any one of these fortresslike condo buildings that sprouted on either side and looked down at the racing freeway traffic below.

Cars rushing in from the left and right. The road peeling away to off-ramps. Pearl Jam's "Animal" on the radio, adding to a sensation in Aisha that she was hunkering down, feeling the old urban paranoia return.

The other three seemed unaffected. They still chatted away, pointing at this or that. But then, they weren't going home after three years' absence.

Home to see a guy who had been her first great love.

She glanced at Christopher. This was her true love now, she reminded herself, and the thought comforted her. She could see Jeff and not feel about him the way she once had. She could talk to Jeff and leave all of that in the past.

She signaled for a lane change but was cut off by a Lexus. She gave the unseeing driver the finger and yelled an obscenity.

"Whoa, Aisha!" It was Lucas, grinning in surprise. "I didn't think you even knew words like that."

"Sorry," she said sheepishly. "Getting back into that urban mentality."

"Why is it that Massachusetts drivers are such jerks?" Christopher asked conversationally.

"It's *Boston* drivers, not everyone from Mass. I think it's the city that drives them insane. It's all narrow little one-way streets going whichever way you *aren't* going."

She cut right and just barely squeezed onto the off-ramp. "Look, um, I was thinking maybe I'd go look around the old neighborhood," Aisha said, as casually as she could. "I thought maybe I'd drop you guys off at Faneuil Hall; you know, you could shop or check out the aquarium."

"She's dumping us," Zoey said to Lucas.

"Oh, yeah, we're being dumped," Lucas agreed good-naturedly.

Christopher looked less inclined to be accepting. Aisha could see resentment clouding his eyes. He gave her a troubled look.

"I just want to look at old places where I grew up," Aisha explained. "You know, a trip down memory lane."

"I guess I would get in your way?" he said.

Aisha reached over and put her hand on his. "Christopher, it's just that this is about my not-very-wonderful past, all right? And you are a big part of my much-more-wonderful present and future, and I guess I feel like I don't want to mix the two up."

"Aw, isn't that sweet?" Lucas said sarcastically from the backseat. He made a gagging noise and Zoey punched him in the arm.

"Okay, babe," Christopher said. "But don't stay too long, okay?"

"I thought what I'd do is park down here by the marketplace. Then I could just take the T around town. I'll meet you guys outside the Orpheum an hour before the show starts." Aisha glanced at her watch. "We meet at the Orpheum at, say, seven? That gives us all a few hours."

She spotted a multistory parking garage and cut across traffic in best Bostonian style.

"What about the costumes?" Zoey asked. "I'm not walking around for the next four hours dressed like a zombie cheerleader."

"Okay, look, I'll leave you guys the keys to the car. I'll go ahead and change into my costume now, and you guys can come back later when you're done shopping."

78

"Zombie cheerleader?" Lucas asked curiously.

"Like a regular cheerleader but with really bad makeup," Zoey said.

"Well, the cheerleader part has potential," Lucas said with a grin.

"And what are you?" Christopher asked Aisha.

Aisha shrugged. "I kind of forgot about the costume thing until the last minute, so I just grabbed my old Girl Scout uniform."

"When was the last time you wore it?" Zoey wondered skeptically.

"When I was fourteen."

"And you still fit into it?"

"It's a little short," Aisha admitted.

"Girl Scout." Christopher shook his head.

"You had a very different experience from me growing up. You could not have walked around my old 'hood dressed that way."

Aisha smiled. "People around my old neighborhood will think they're having a flashback. It will be just like three years ago, Aisha Gray walking around in her Girl Scout uniform with her merit badges, selling cookies."

"This is insane," Claire muttered to herself. "Insane, and now it's annoying, too."

The rain was coming down hard by the time Claire hit the outskirts of Boston. The rain was falling and the rush-hour traffic had brought everything to a dead stop. At the moment, she was staring out past her windshield wipers at a sea of wet cars, all sitting motionless. Occasionally there would be a frustration explosion and horns would start going off. Then they would all move ahead fifty feet and stop again.

She checked the dashboard clock. Still plenty of time to make it to the airport, but she had wanted to get there early—early enough to be there before "Flyer," who would undoubtedly also show up early for their strange blind date.

In some ways the rain was a godsend. If she decided to bail out of the meeting, she could say that the rain had delayed her. Too bad it wasn't snowing.

Claire looked at the small sheaf of papers on the seat beside her. This was probably an insane thing to do. Why would she want to meet a person she knew only from a computer billboard?

She knew the answer, of course. In a strange way Flyer—Sean—had become a big part of her life, filling a hole that had become ever more obvious as she found herself more and more isolated, more and more alone.

"Pathetic," she told herself roughly. "Nina would laugh herself into a coma if she knew."

She picked up the top few sheets of paper. They were printouts of her last AOL conversation with Flyer.

FLYER

I meant what I said yesterday. I know I can only judge you by what you've written me over the short time we've communicated, WG. But I like you a lot.

WEATHERGIRL

You don't even know me.

FLYER

I think I do, in a way. For one thing, I know you without being distracted by how you look.

WEATHERGIRL

What do you think I look like?

80

FLYER

I guess I don't really care that much. I
suppose that's the point.

WEATHERGIRL

What if I'm extremely unattractive?

A horn sounded right behind her, and Claire looked
up from the paper to see that the traffic had moved
twenty feet. She took her foot off the brake and crept up
to fill in the gap.

FLYER

Again, I don't care. It's you the person I
like. Unless you've just been lying the
whole time, I see you as a very smart,
private, reflective person. I also think
you're lonely. And maybe that feeling of
loneliness causes you to be hard with
people sometimes.

Claire smiled faintly. That wasn't an image of Claire
that any of her friends, let alone her sister, would agree
with. Everyone else thought she was just an ice princess,
given to manipulation, selfishness, and even ruthlessness.

Frankly, Claire thought, the truth lay somewhere between Flyer's rosy vision and Nina's less flattering ver-
sion. Was she lonely? Maybe that wasn't far from being
true. Especially lately. It had been driven home by the
way she had managed to lose Jake.

She glanced at the conversation again.

FLYER

What if it turns out that I'm the
unattractive one?

81

WEATHERGIRL

I've never cared much about looks either.

FLYER

I have a proposition, WG. If you don't
want to do it, then just say so. No
pressure. You know I just got my pilot's
license, and I thought I might fly over
there to Maine to see you, or else maybe
we could meet at some neutral spot somewhere.

WEATHERGIRL

I'm not so sure that's a good idea. Maybe
in person we wouldn't get along as well as
we do here.

FLYER

Maybe we'd get along even better. Aren't
you curious?

WEATHERGIRL

I'll admit I am curious. I've talked more
with you than I have with anyone in a long
time.

More than anyone since she'd broken up with Benjamin, Claire realized. Jake had never been one for long
conversations.

FLYER

Okay, how about this: Halloween is
tomorrow. The perfect day for people who
may not fit the standard definition of
beauty. Meet me on Halloween.

Halloween? Where?

Somewhere public, so you can feel safe.
Somewhere we can both get to that's a
neutral spot. And then, if we meet and
don't like each other, fine. We go our
separate ways.

I'm supposed to go to a concert in Boston
on Halloween. Maybe if I left here early,
we could spend a little time together.

They had decided on the airport as the logical place
to get together. Flyer—Sean—would be flying in, Claire
would be driving past. It was perfect. Logan Airport was
a big, well-lit, safe place on neutral turf. A place where,
if she decided to, she could bail at the last minute and
melt into the crowds. And with the concert, Claire had
the perfect excuse to run for it early if things went bad
between her and Sean.

Nina

Halloween, the Season of fear! Boo! Ha ha ha ha. Okay, you want to know what scares me? How about the possibility that I may wake up someday and find I actually like a Mariah Carey song? Okay, no, my real fear is that I may someday see Rush Limbaugh at the beach! In a thong! No! The horror! Wait, worse: I'm kidnapped by a cult that forces me to buy all my clothes at Papagallo's! Someone hold my hand, please. I'm frightened.

Seriously, though, what am I afraid of? I'll tell you, though even speaking about it gives me the willies. It's...it's the creature who lives upstairs from my room. Oh, I know you're laughing. I know you're thinking 'Nina, there is no creature living above your room; grow up.' But I assure you there is: a cold, ruthless monster! A destroyer of souls! Dare I speak the monster's name aloud? Yes, its name is Claire, which in Transylvanian means "ice princess with overly large breasts and no heart."

Those Transylvanians know how to load a single word up with meaning, don't they?

Eleven

"Why am I feeling bumps?" Benjamin demanded.

"Okay, I'll play along," Nina said. "Why are you feeling bumps?"

"My butt tells me this is not the highway. That last pothole was not an interstate highway type of bump. That was a crappy little back road kind of bump."

Nina looked around at the fields on either side of the road. Plowed-up dirt turning to mud as the rain saturated the ground. Deep ditches on either side of the definitely crappy little back road were turning into streams.

"It's a shortcut," Nina explained as the van hit another shockingly deep pothole.

"Wait a minute. Doesn't the highway run almost straight from Weymouth to Boston?"

"Yeah, but how about rush hour? This will take us past all the traffic."

Nina turned on the radio, but the storm clouds overhead had fuzzed out all but a mournful country music station. She should have thought to bring tapes. The only cassettes available were from Benjamin and Zoey's mom. Simon and Garfunkel.

"Let me ask you something, Nina," Benjamin said. "What state are we in?"

"What state?" Nina looked around, trying to peer

through the gloom. "Mmm, New Hampshire?"

"Oh, man, we're lost, aren't we?"

"Lost?" Nina shrugged. "How could we be lost? We're right here on this road."

"Which road?"

"You mean like a number?"

Benjamin shook his head. "Great. Well, at least there's a chance we'll miss the concert now. There's always that silver lining."

"We are not going to miss anything," Nina said. "Every road goes somewhere."

"Yeah. *The road goes ever on and on, down from the door where it began. Now far ahead the road has gone, and I must follow if I can . . .* "

"Cool. What's that, poetry?"

"It's from *The Lord of the Rings*."

"Well, see, like you said, the road goes on and on and it has to lead somewhere eventually."

"In *Lord of the Rings* it led to Mordor," Benjamin muttered darkly.

"What's Mordor?" Nina wondered distractedly.

"It's kind of like parts of New York City, from what I understand," Benjamin said dryly.

"Okay," Nina said cheerfully, "so we'll go to New York." It was a good thing Benjamin couldn't see, because the road had grown narrower and now, instead of plowed fields on either side, there were more and more trees, towering pines that crowded out what little light had penetrated the clouds. Soon, Nina realized, true night would fall, and without streetlights or moonlight this road would be invisible beyond the small circle of the headlights.

Maybe after she looked around the next curve in the road she should just admit she was lost and turn the van around and go back. Although there would be no way to hide that fact from Benjamin. He would certainly know they were turning around.

Nina flipped on the lights.

"Is it dark?" Benjamin asked.

Nina sighed. "You heard the switch?"

"Of course."

Nina sighed again.

"Okay, Nina, how lost are we?"

"Well, Benjamin, we're surrounded by trees, it's getting dark, I haven't seen a house or a mailbox in a long, long time, and this road is looking more and more like it might be dirt real soon."

Benjamin took this news calmly. "Why don't we turn around?"

"We can try, but the road is so narrow and all. And there's ditches on either side. Oh, wait, we're at a field. I think I see a spot to turn around up ahead."

Nina hunkered over the wheel, peering ahead. Yes, the trees had opened up on one side, revealing a field. And there was a tiny dirt track leading away from the main road. That would be the place to turn around and race back to civilization.

She applied brakes and turned onto the dirt road. She stopped, put the gearshift in reverse, turned around and looked back over her shoulder, and stepped lightly on the gas.

There was a wild spinning sound. The van rocked and didn't move.

"Uh-oh."

She stepped on the gas again. More spinning, and she could just make out a plume of mud being thrown forward by the wheels.

The rain had caught up with Aisha soon after she exited the T station. But her coat had a nice hood that kept her hair dry and her upper body warm. It also hid the

Girl Scout costume, which looked a little ridiculous for just walking around town in the evening.

She had lived in the south end back in those days. It wasn't one of Boston's more famous neighborhoods. It wasn't Back Bay or Beacon Hill or Southie. The south end was an area of close-packed bow-front Victorian town homes. Working class for the most part, people who drove cabs or worked as nurses or secretaries. There were bad streets, streets you didn't walk down at night, where cars had no hubcaps and sometimes no wheels and the bars over the windows were starkly functional. And other streets where the buildings had been occupied by invading yuppies who stripped the chipped green paint from their massive front doors and polished the oak beneath. People who hung stained-glass windows and parked Lexuses out front.

She passed the reflecting pool, a long rectangle where in summer she and other kids from the neighborhood had waded to beat the heat.

She walked along West Newton, fighting the wet wind that lifted the tail of her coat and tried to pull off her hood. On a nicer day people would have been out on their stoops, watching the passing show. But the rain had emptied the streets of everyone but the few commuters heading home early.

She had two goals in mind. First was to see her old home, a narrow, drafty Victorian virtually identical to dozens on either side. The second goal was to see Jeff's house.

She didn't know why she wanted to see his home. She didn't even know if he still lived there with his mother and his odd collection of aunts. Perhaps nowadays Jeff was making enough money to be able to buy or rent a better place. The Pullings' home had always been one of the shabbier ones, a stark contrast to the Grays' restored bow front, where Aisha's mother had first discovered her fascination with decorating.

Aisha found her own home easily, of course. It was dark and silent. The new owners had added a piece of stained glass that Aisha was pretty certain her mother would hate. It was odd and even disturbing somehow to stand there in the rain, wearing her fourteen-year-old's Girl Scout uniform and experiencing this imperfect mix of the familiar and the strange. Somehow she'd expected a more cosmic experience.

But as she stared thoughtfully at the house some memories did surface, happy for the most part. Some melancholy. In the gray drizzle it was hard somehow to hold on to the happy ones. She remembered the names of her friends in those days. Lachandra, a hopelessly giddy girl who had been boy-crazy since she was eleven. Anna Maria, who at the age of fourteen had begun to see things and hear things that no one else did and had ended up being packed off to a mental hospital, from which she sent strange, self-pitying letters. And Kinya, Aisha's best friend until Jeff had come between them.

Aisha walked on, head bowed. Her feet directed her without conscious thought, down the street to the corner and right. She looked up at one point, surprised to see that she was halfway to Jeff's house. She even remembered the shortcut, down the alley.

What would she say to Jeff if he was at his old house? To know *that* she'd have to figure out how she felt about him, which was something she wasn't sure of, even now. She knew she loved Christopher. But did that necessarily mean she no longer cared at all for Jeff?

"Hey, sister."

Aisha looked up, breaking from her reverie. She was in the alley, surrounded by blank brick walls. Ahead of her were two men. At least she assumed they were men. They both wore rubber Halloween masks. One was a gorilla, the other President Clinton. For a moment she wondered if the guy in the Clinton mask was Christopher. It was the same mask, but this person was younger and smaller.

Aisha clutched her purse instinctively. On Chatham Island or even for the most part in Weymouth there would have been nothing to be concerned about. But this was the big city. In Boston chance encounters with strangers in alleyways were not to be encouraged.

"Hey, sister," the gorilla called again, drawing nearer.

Aisha glanced over her shoulder. A long way back to the main street.

"You can't talk?" President Clinton asked.

Aisha felt her stomach muscles clenching tight. She forced a smile. "Hi."

They were coming closer with each step. Aisha felt the hairs on the back of her neck standing on end. Somewhere she could hear music playing. Madonna, of all things. A song she had liked when she'd lived in this very neighborhood.

The guys in the masks were just ahead. Level with her. Now behind her.

Aisha breathed a sigh of relief.

Suddenly she was spun around by the force of someone yanking hard on her purse. She held on and yelled, "No!"

A mistake, she knew. She should have let them take the purse. There was no chance of her being saved by anyone, and the smart thing to do was let them have it.

The gorilla yanked again at her purse. The man in the Clinton mask slapped her hard with the back of his hand. In shock Aisha released the purse. And now Gorilla pushed her viciously.

She slipped and fell backward. Her head struck hard against the brick wall. She fell to the ground. She heard laughter and saw a band of dark gray sky.

Then she lost consciousness.

Twelve

It was full night as Claire pulled into short-term parking at the airport. She glanced at her watch. By the time she made her way from the parking lot to the terminal building, she'd barely be on time for the meeting, let alone early enough to spy the situation out safely.

She was beginning to bitterly regret having agreed to the meeting. What on earth had possessed her to say yes? For that matter, what on earth had possessed her to begin this weird computer friendship with some guy?

It wasn't like there was a shortage of guys at school. There were guys who would have sold their parents into slavery for the opportunity to go out with Claire Geiger.

Yes, she had been feeling resentful and hurt. Had felt unloved and even disliked. Cut off from everyone she knew. Lonely. Deserted. Yes, yes, all that, but that was no reason to start forming relationships with people who were nothing more than words on a monitor screen.

"I'll take a look," she told herself. "Anything looks wrong, I'm out of there, and I just stay off America Online in the future."

Claire checked herself in the rearview mirror and pulled a brush from her purse. She brushed her glossy, long black hair while checking her minimal makeup. Still fine.

She ran through the scattered raindrops to the terminal building. Inside she bought a *USA Today* at a newsstand. It would help her to fit in, to look unobtrusive. She found the restaurant easily, following the signs, and quickly scanned the dozen or so occupied tables. No one who stood out obviously as Flyer. The only person of the right age was a hugely fat guy sitting with another person whose back was turned to her.

Claire nodded in satisfaction. Now she would just grab a bench across the breezeway and watch who came and went in the restaurant. With a little luck she would be able to spot Flyer. After all, how many unaccompanied seventeen-year-old guys were likely to be at this airport, on this concourse, at this restaurant, at the right time?

Yes, she would surely be able to spot him. And then . . . and then she'd decide what to do.

She unfolded the newspaper, holding it up to conceal her face. She was deciphering a bar graph on the number of Americans who ate particular types of cheese when she became aware of someone standing nearby.

Reluctantly, and fearing the worst, she lowered the paper and raised her eyes.

He was six feet tall, broad shouldered, wearing a worn brown leather jacket and nicely fitted Levi's. He had shoulder-length blond hair, a perfect nose, a lopsided smile that revealed perfect white teeth. His eyes were a pale, slightly vacant blue, his only minor flaw.

Claire reminded herself that she didn't care what Flyer looked like. Didn't care at all.

"Weathergirl?" he said.

"Flyer?" she asked, standing up.

"Well, well," he said. "I mean, um . . . obviously you are one of those rare people whose inner beauty is fully reflected in their outer appearance."

Claire realized to her amazement that she was blushing. All the guys she had gone out with were good looking, but this guy was male-model good looking. Not that she cared. Flyer pushed the hair back out of his eyes, and Claire caught sight of something on his right ear. He acknowledged the direction of her gaze with a smile.

"A hearing aid," he said. "The result of a regrettable carelessness with firecrackers when I was even younger and dumber than I am today. It's why I've been a little nervous about meeting you face-to-face. I wasn't sure what you'd think."

Like I would run screaming from the room because you have a hearing aid? Claire asked silently. Aloud she said, "I couldn't care less. I'm just glad to meet you."

A guy this beautiful *and* this smart and he'd just been waiting around to be picked up on a computer billboard? Something told Claire the odds were way, way against it.

He smiled with his perfect teeth. "I feel like I already know you so well," he said.

Jake had pulled the quick cut, as islanders called it.

The outbound ferry went from Weymouth to Chatham Island, then on to the outer islands of Allworthy and Penobscot. On the return it stopped again at Chatham Island on its way back to the mainland.

There were forty-five minutes between the outward-bound ferry and the inbound ferry. Jake had caught the regular four o'clock home from school, arriving at Chatham Island at four twenty-five. Then he had gone from the ferry to his home, drunk his father's last three beers, picked up what he needed, and caught the five ten going back across to the mainland.

It was raining on the return leg, so he sat below on the covered deck. In a corner by himself he pulled the license out of his pocket and looked at it. It was something he'd kept these last two years since his brother Wade's death—Wade's driver's license. He had never consciously admitted why he was hanging on to it, but a part of his mind had known that the day would come when it would be useful.

He peered closely at the date of birth. How Wade had gotten it done, he didn't know, but the alteration was just about perfect. Someone would have to look very closely to see that the year of birth had been changed, making a five into a three. Of course, if Wade had lived, he'd actually be twenty-one soon.

Someone sat beside him and he started guiltily, covering the license with his hand.

A girl. She looked vaguely familiar, as if he'd seen her somewhere quite recently. Then it came to him. She had been on the outbound ferry just like him, and done the same quick cut. He narrowed his eyes suspiciously. He knew everyone on Chatham Island, and it was no longer tourist season. Besides, this girl wasn't dressed like a tourist. She had on a painfully short skirt over fishnet stockings and high, black leather boots. Her hair was brown and she wore it big. Underneath a cheap black leather jacket with too many zippers she had on an incongruous tube top.

She was looking at him as suspiciously as he watched her.

"Can I help you?" Jake said at last.

"I was just wondering," she said.

"Okay," he said guardedly.

"I went to see if I could find someone on the island. But there are more houses there than I thought. I thought it would just be like a few houses and I wouldn't have any problem."

"Who were you looking for?"

"This guy." She stared at him, as if anticipating a reaction. "This *blind* guy."

"Benjamin?"

She nodded. "Yeah, that's his name. Funny you should know right off like that."

"There's only one blind person on the island," Jake said. "The whole population is only three hundred, so it's not like they could sneak a new blind guy on without me noticing it."

It had been a joke. A feeble joke, but the girl seemed alarmed. "They?"

"Never mind," Jake said. "So you're looking for Benjamin. He's out of town tonight. Him and his sister both, they went to Boston for a concert."

The girl leaned close. Jake could smell perfume, hair spray, and cigarette smoke. "*I'm* his sister," she said.

"Excuse me?"

"I'm the blind boy's sister," she said. "His *other* sister."

"Okay," Jake said, humoring her.

"You don't believe me?" the girl asked craftily. "Well, I am. I found out last week."

It finally clicked in Jake's mind. Of course. What a relief; he had been starting to wonder if the girl was crazy, which would be a shame, because underneath the sleazy clothes and overly thick makeup she wasn't at all bad looking. "I get it now," he said. "You're the famous half sister."

"Famous?" she demanded.

"Well, not exactly famous," Jake backpedaled. "We all know each other on the island, so naturally I know that Benjamin and Zoey have . . . have you."

"Who's Zoey?"

"Benjamin's sister. Or, I guess she's also your half sister," he said. "Your name is Lara, right?"

She smiled suddenly, unexpectedly. "Lara McAvoy."

He stuck out his hand. "Jake. Jake McRoyan. We both have 'Mc' names. You, me, and McDonald's."

His earlier joke might have fallen flat, but this one

caused a sudden, loud outburst of wild laughter. Lara laughed so hard that Jake couldn't help but join in.

She stopped at last and looked at him with her oddly direct gaze. "What are you doing tonight, Jake?"

Jake shrugged. He'd been planning on using Wade's old driver's license to buy a case of beer, then find a nice, comfortable place to drink it. Halloween night there would be parties going on in Portside Weymouth, and carrying a case of beer he'd be welcome almost anywhere a party was under way.

"I was just trying to decide what to do," he said. Then in a burst of frankness, "I was thinking seriously about getting drunk."

Lara nodded solemnly. "That's good. That's good. I like to get drunk, too. My boyfriend and I usually get drunk together, but he's in jail tonight."

"Jail?"

Lara shrugged. "He can't get his bail reduced until Thursday."

"What did he do?" Jake asked, not sure he wanted to know.

"I'm not supposed to tell," Lara said, putting a finger to her lips. "Can you get anything to drink?" she asked him.

Jake held out the license sheepishly. "I think I can."

Lara stared at it, her eyes wide. "That's a dead person," she said.

Jake felt a thrill go up his spine. "How do you know that?" he demanded.

But Lara only smiled dreamily. "Come and get drunk with me. Then you can tell me about my blind brother."

JAKE

Wow. What am I afraid of? I'm
not afraid of physical pain or
anything like that. You play
football, you get used to
physical pain. The only thing I'm
afraid of is that I might be
weak sometime. You know? Like
I'm starting to think maybe I'm
an alcoholic or something, and
I'm afraid of anything like that
where it would be about me
being weak. I don't like being
out of control.

Of course you'd say, well,
Jake, when you drink too much
you are out of control, right?
Only it's not like that. Getting
drunk makes me feel like I
_am_ in control. When you're

drunk, you're not afraid of anything.

At least that's the way it seems.

Thirteen

Faneuil Hall Marketplace was a gigantic affair. Three long, narrow buildings, each almost two football fields in length, lay parallel to one another, separated by open plazas lined with outdoor cafés and pushcart vendors selling everything from T-shirts to pepper gas spray.

In the summer it was a madhouse. Even now, on a rainy autumn evening with a chilly breeze blowing from the bay, it was packed inside, though the only outdoor cafés in operation were those with plastic enclosures.

Zoey, Lucas, and Christopher sat in one of these, chilly but determined to eat alfresco. Night was falling fast, but the rain had let up. Overhead there were even occasional glimpses of dark sky through the clouds. Zoey was halfway through a crab salad that cost eleven ninety-five, about twice what was charged at her parents' restaurant. Lucas had finished his burger and Christopher had consumed a pair of sautéed soft shells, offering expert criticism on their freshness and preparation to the point where both Zoey and Lucas were getting sick of him.

Before dinner they had changed into their Halloween costumes, and Zoey was disguised with death-blue makeup on her face, bare legs, and hands. A fairly realistic plastic ax was half-buried in her head, completing the zombie cheerleader costume. For the two guys "costume" meant nothing more than masks, which lay on the table.

Lucas was looking at her and shaking his head in amusement. "I always figured you more for a Snow White, princess kind of thing," he said. "But I like this. The combination of that whole cheerleader sexiness thing with the zombie thing counterbalancing it."

Zoey gave him a steely look. "You think cheerleaders are sexy?"

"Did I say that?" Lucas looked alarmed.

"You just said 'that whole cheerleader sexiness thing,' " Zoey said.

"You're in it now, man," Christopher said in an aside.

"I just meant that on you the cheerleader thing was sexy," Lucas said.

"Uh-huh. What exactly is it you guys like about cheerleaders?"

"I don't care about cheerleaders one way or the other," Christopher said. "All I care about is Aisha. And I'm not just saying that because I know you'll report that back to her when we see her later."

"Well, at least I managed to have a full costume, unlike you two," Zoey said.

"We have masks," Lucas said defensively.

"Big deal, masks. I had to put blue makeup all the way up my legs. You guys just pull on your monkey masks or whatever and that's it."

"*All* the way up your legs?" Lucas asked.

"I guess you won't find that out unless I do a somersault," Zoey said, batting her eyes. "And I'm not sure that zombie cheerleaders actually do the more acrobatic cheers. My point is, I put some effort into it, unlike you two slackers."

"I offered to help with the makeup," Lucas said wolfishly.

"Girls are into dress-up, unlike us manly men," Christopher said. "Although actually, as soon as I said that I realized Aisha didn't exactly go to much trouble. Just her old Girl Scout costume. What's Nina doing for a costume?"

Zoey grinned at the memory. "She got ahold of a long black wig and swiped some of Claire's clothing. Then she's going to stuff her bra with like eight pairs of socks."

"She's going as Claire?" Lucas asked. "Cute."

"Who is going to know that she's supposed to be Claire?" Christopher asked.

"Well, she says she's going to hand out cards that say 'for a good time call Claire,' with their phone number on it." Zoey made a back-and-forth gesture with her hand. "I don't know if she'll really go through with that part, though. Benjamin is going to be the devil. Nina says they'll be a natural couple: Mr. and Mrs. Satan."

Lucas glanced at his watch. "Have to get going soon."

"Yeah," Christopher agreed. "Besides, it's no fun being the single guy hanging around with you two. I need my little Girl Scout. Even if she *did* ditch me."

"Oh, Christopher, you know how it is. She probably wanted to hook up with her old girlfriends from when she lived here and tell them all about you. How could she do that if you were there?" Zoey said.

Christopher brightened amazingly. "Yeah, that must be it."

Zoey looked down at the check to conceal her grin. Guys. Appeal to their ego and they would believe anything.

*　　*　　*

Aisha groaned and opened her eyes. Her head throbbed painfully, and she reached to touch it. Only then did she realize that she was lying on her side. The cold, wet ground had numbed her left arm and leg. Her coat was soaked and sodden where it touched the ground, but a slight overhang of the eaves above her had kept her out of the direct rainfall.

She struggled to sit up. Pins and needles burned extravagantly as blood rushed back into her left arm and leg. She tried to stand, but with no feeling in one leg it was impossible. She leaned back against the brick wall. When her head touched the wall, she realized instantly that a large lump had risen. It was concealed by her hair, but her fingers found it and confirmed a bump practically the size of a golf ball.

She looked curiously at her surroundings. Where was she, and how had she ended up here?

It looked like the alleyway she usually took to get to Jeff's house. But how had she gotten this bump on the head? And what was she doing lying on the wet ground?

She opened her coat and saw that she was wearing her uniform. The hem of the skirt was soaked.

With feeling returning to her leg and arm, she made a second attempt to stand up. This was successful, although her head still felt as if it might explode.

She looked down at her skirt. For some reason it seemed amazingly short. Certainly it hadn't always been that short, had it? Or had it shrunk somehow? Maybe from getting wet? That didn't make any sense, but what other explanation was there?

She wrung the water out of the skirt's hem and out of the coat. She was very cold. Cold and stiff and strangely confused, unable to recall why she had been going down the alley.

Perhaps, she reasoned, the bump on her head had discombobulated her a little. Maybe she should see a doctor or something. Then she remembered: Jeff's mother was a nurse. She'd obviously been on her way there anyway. But what would Mrs. Pullings say about this uniform? And the way she was all wet?

"Okay, Aisha," she told herself. "Get a grip, girl. You were on your way to Jeff's house and you slipped and banged into the wall."

The sound of her voice, though strangely low, comforted her. Obviously her brain was working, and now that the numbness was gone she could move all her limbs, so no big deal. Everything was cool.

She certainly didn't want to go running home to her parents and tell them. Her mother would ask what she was doing in that alleyway when she'd told her daughter a million times to stay out of alleys. Her mother would know she was on her way to be with Jeff, and that whole fight would start up all over again. Then her mother would start in about leaving Boston and finding some nice, peaceful place where bad things never happened and there were no older guys chasing her daughter.

She began trudging down the alley. *See*, she told herself self-righteously, this *is what happens when Mother treats me like a child*. Now she couldn't even tell her mother that she'd hurt herself for fear of how her mother would overreact.

It was ridiculous. After all, she was fourteen years old and plenty mature enough to decide who she would go out with and even what she would do with Jeff, the guy she loved with all her heart.

"Okay, punch it!" Benjamin yelled. He leaned all his weight against the front of the van, digging his shoes into the soft, wet earth.

Nina pressed down on the gas. The front wheels spun backward, making a futile sound and spraying mud forward. After a few seconds she stopped and peered over the wheel. In the brilliant glare of the headlights Benjamin looked almost frightening. His jeans, his jacket, and one side of his face were plastered with mud. He stood there calmly, removed his shades, and squeegeed the mud off with a finger.

Nina rolled down the window and stuck out her head. "I suppose you blame me for all this?"

"No, no," Benjamin said, shaking mud off his sleeve. "There were two of us in the van when we were getting lost. Of course, one of us can't see, but still and all, I accept my part of the blame for getting lost out somewhere . . ." He shrugged helplessly. "Somewhere in the woods of either Maine, New Hampshire, or Massachusetts."

"I'm almost positive it isn't Vermont," Nina said helpfully. "So, we've narrowed it down to just three states."

Benjamin reached out to touch the front of the van. He felt his way around to the window. "Give me a kiss, and make it good," he demanded with mock severity.

Nina wiped mud from his lips and kissed him.

"Sorry we're slightly lost," Nina said.

"And stuck in the mud," Benjamin added.

"That too."

He found his way around to the passenger door and climbed in. "Well."

"You know," Nina said, "this dirt road must lead somewhere."

"This *mud* road," Benjamin corrected.

"Whatever. But someone put it here for a reason. There's probably a farm down there. Somewhere. We can go to the farm and call a tow truck."

"Yeah, we'll just tell him we're somewhere in one of three possible states."

"At least it's not raining right now," Nina pointed out.

"Oh, right, that is a huge blessing. Thank God there's no rain or I might be able to wash off some of this mud."

"If we're going to go find the farmhouse, we might as well go now while it's not raining," Nina said. "A ten-minute walk, we call a tow truck, and we still make the concert on time."

"On what planet?" Benjamin said darkly.

Nina crawled into the back of the van. "Let me see if your folks keep a flashlight in here."

"Is it dark?" Benjamin asked.

"Between the clouds and the fact that it's like getting kind of late, and the sun goes down at five this time of year, yes, it's dark out."

"Well, don't be scared," Benjamin said, softening. "The dark is nothing."

Easy for you to say, Nina thought. Frankly, to her the dark—the starless, moonless dark, the rural, backwoods, no city lights, no car headlights, no reflected TV glow kind of total dark—was utterly unnerving.

But she couldn't start acting scared. Once you started acting scared, you just got more scared. Like when you'd walk faster past a graveyard or something, and the faster you walked the more you became convinced that something . . . something hideous and terrible was following you, chasing you with evil eyes glowing, sharp teeth—

"Here!" Nina said loudly. "A flashlight." She snapped it on. To her utter relief the light came on strong, casting sharp, dancing shadows around the inside of the van.

"Okay, let's go. Now at least one of us can see," she announced, trying to sound confident.

"I'll have to hold on to your arm," Benjamin said apologetically.

"I can live with that," Nina said. "But you have to carry the bag."

"What bag?"

"My backpack. I have my purse and our costumes in there."

"Costumes? You figure we'll have to trick-or-treat out here?"

"It's cold; we might appreciate any extra clothes we can get," Nina pointed out.

Outside on the road she let his hand close around her right arm. In her left hand she held the flashlight, playing it down the path, down what she fervently *hoped* was a long driveway. The beam illuminated the first few dozen yards of gravel, just to the point where the track veered left, away from the open field and into the trees.

They set off together, feet crunching on wet gravel. In ten steps the van was invisible. Darkness closed around them, hemming them in, blanking out everything but the unworldly bluish light from the flash.

"I hope it's got those bunny batteries," Nina muttered.

"What?"

"Nothing. Quiet, isn't it?"

"Very," Benjamin agreed. "That's good," he added. "I'd hear if there was something dangerous."

"Like what?" Nina demanded sharply.

"Nothing. Bears. I don't know."

"Bears? Try insane serial killers," Nina said. They had reached the line of the trees. She stopped. "We're at the trees. I think maybe the farmhouse will be right around the corner."

"Okay."

Nina tried to shine the light through the trees, but the undergrowth and the tightly ranked tree trunks swallowed the beam. Now there was the sound of dripping. Rainwater dripping from a thousand tree limbs. Then a shockingly loud hoot.

"Damn!" Nina cried.

"What?"

"Didn't you hear it?"

"What, the bird?" Benjamin said.

"Bird?"

"Yeah, it was an owl, Nina." Benjamin laughed. "*You* just worry about what can be seen. I'll let you know if there's anything that can be heard."

"Deal," Nina said shakily.

They advanced again, taking small steps, close together, Nina playing the beam back and forth from the woods on one side to the woods on the other side.

Benjamin suddenly tightened his grip on her arm and pulled her to a stop.

"What?"

"Shh," he said. "Listen."

"If you are playing games with me, Benjamin, I swear—"

"Quiet!"

She shone the light on his face. His head was tilted sideways, listening intently.

"Violin," he said at last. "I thought it might be a viola, but I'm sure it's a violin."

"A violin? *What's* a violin?"

"That music. Can't you hear it? Someone's playing Bach."

"I don't care if they're playing Monopoly," Nina said, breathing a sigh of relief. She listened herself now and could just make out the thin, distant sound. "Anyone with a violin must have a phone."

Fourteen

"Do you want to go into the restaurant?" Claire asked.

Tables were emptying out now as more flights were called. The fat guy was still there, although his companion was gone. For some reason this seemed significant to some corner of Claire's mind.

"No, it's pretty crappy, really," Flyer said.

Claire smiled at him. "Crappy?"

"I mean it's . . ." He paused. "Okay, let's go in and have a seat. I think that would be great."

They were given a table by the windows. Night had fallen. Colored runway lights cast long red lines across the wet tarmac. Just outside, a Delta 727 waited to take on passengers. Farther out a United jet roared down the runway and disappeared beyond the range of Claire's vision.

"What can I get you?" Flyer asked.

"Coffee, I suppose."

"So." Flyer smiled gorgeously. "Shall we go on calling each other Weathergirl and Flyer, or may I use your real name?"

"I guess real names would make more sense."

"Claire," he said, savoring the word. "I remember that you told me it might not be your real name, that perhaps you had just made it up, but I knew instantly that it was real. It fit perfectly. As soon as I saw it show up on my screen I felt a chill of recognition. Like, yes, of course it's *Claire*.''

Claire gulped and was glad for the arrival of the coffee as a distraction. Flyer was so much more than she had expected. It was almost overwhelming. The guys she'd gone out with in the past were people she'd grown up with. Handsome, yes, but familiar. This guy, this guy whose mind she knew well before she'd ever had the first sight of him, was like some vision of perfection. So smart, so charming, *and* so good looking?

And he liked her. Even after she had confessed so much to him.

''I'd like it if you called me Claire,'' she said. '' 'Weathergirl' seems a little strange for two people sharing a cup of coffee. And can I call you Sean?''

He grinned again, and again Claire felt an answering glow.

''You remember? I'm flattered.''

''Of course I remember . . . Sean,'' Claire said.

''So,'' he said.

''So,'' she said.

''I guess this is our first awkward pause,'' Sean said.

''Mmm-hmm.''

''We never had these when we were typing to each other,'' he said.

''No. I guess that's because we . . .'' She shrugged. ''Well, it's different face-to-face.''

''I suppose it is,'' he agreed. ''Although you always said that appearances didn't matter.''

Claire grinned wryly. ''I did say that, didn't I?''

''I mean, it's really your mind and what you believe and think that has meaning for me,'' Sean said. He raised an eyebrow as if he disapproved of what he had just said.

''Well, I feel the same,'' Claire said. ''I mean, really.

I guess we're friends, in a way. I don't know; it's confusing, isn't it?"

"Is it?"

"I mean, I think of you as someone I know. We've had what, maybe a dozen or so conversations, and in some ways I've been more honest with you than I am with people I really know." She shook her head. "But see? I say *people I really know*, and by that I just mean people I've seen in person."

"This is something of an undiscovered country, isn't it?" Sean said, looking thoughtful. "Friendships that are formed between people who have only met through a computer screen."

"Like pen pals in the old days," Claire suggested.

"Exactly. That's right; I'd forgotten that people used to have pen pals. So all we've done is update things. We can interact more. Instead of me sending a letter one week and you writing back the next week and so on, we can write back and forth instantly. Still . . . there is the same big moment when the pen pals or computer friends meet in person."

"In the flesh," Claire said. She instantly regretted the choice of words, especially when, as if on cue, Sean's eyes dipped to the green silk stretched over her breasts. That was definitely new, she told herself. "Flyer" couldn't give her looks like the one Sean had just given her.

Not that she resented it. It was just different.

"I have to, uh, run to the little boys' room," Sean said.

"I'll wait," Claire said.

He stood up, and with a last smile that had the same dazzling effect as his earlier smiles, he turned and walked away.

Claire sipped her coffee. With as much casual disinterest as she could manage, she eyed his form threading

111

its way through the tables. Nice form. Very nice form. Yes, despite her best intentions, things were different when bodies were involved as well as minds.

She followed him till he disappeared, aware that she was smiling slightly, and not caring. Her gaze drifted away, and for a moment she caught the eye of the fat kid, still sitting, hunched over a book. Probably waiting for a delayed flight. Claire let her usual curtain of disdain settle over her face, feeling embarrassed to be caught leering openly at a guy's tightly jeaned butt.

Now, while Sean was away, was the perfect opportunity for her to bail out if she wanted to.

Only, she definitely didn't want to.

Jake wiped his palms on his jeans and ran his hand through his hair. He glanced over at Lara. She was standing by the pay phone outside the convenience store, smoking a cigarette and looking tough and nonchalant.

He shrugged and went inside. He blinked like a mole in the fluorescent glare, then took a quick look at the clerk. A middle-aged guy, thin, ridiculous in a too-small, stained blazer.

He passed down the candy aisle, going straight for the cooler. There was no point in pretending he was really there for chewing gum and the beer was some kind of an afterthought. That was stupid. He was there for beer, and the sooner he tried to buy it, the sooner he would know if the man in the blazer would accept his fake ID.

But just to show that he was cool and calm and it was all no big deal, he did bend down and pick up a bag of Doritos. Then he went to the beer cases at the back of the store.

He pulled out two twelve-packs of Bud, balancing the chips on top, and made his way back to the counter. A woman in front of him was buying lottery tickets and taking her time.

The rain had made his jacket damp, and now he found he was both cold and sweaty simultaneously. He adopted a blank, slightly impatient expression and stared at the *National Enquirer* and the *Weekly World News*. Apparently a chemical plant explosion in Louisiana had released a cloud of smoke that showed Elvis in mortal combat with the devil.

He reached the counter at last and hefted the beer up onto the high counter.

"Sorry, but I have to see some ID."

Jake smiled. "Sure. No problem." He dug out his wallet and slid out the license.

The man looked closely at the license. Then at Jake. "Wade McRoyan, huh?"

"Yes," Jake said. "That's me."

"Name sounds familiar."

Jake tried not to show any sign of panic. This guy remembered his brother? It wasn't impossible. Wade had been a big high school football star, and high school football was one of the few sports in the area. And then, too, his death, the accident, had made the news.

"Lots of guys named Wade," Jake said lamely.

A smile flickered on the man's thin lips. He handed the license back to Jake and rang up the purchase.

Jake breathed a huge sigh of relief as he passed through the doors to the outside. Lara came sidling over, tossing her cigarette on the ground. She didn't offer to help carry the beer but sauntered off, past a carload of partygoers dressed in costume and playing Metallica at ground-pounding intensity.

She led him to the four-story brick building on Independence, two blocks away. He followed her up the stairs, to the fourth floor, where she extracted her keys and unlocked the door.

It was dark inside.

"This is it," she said.

"Looks great so far," Jake said dryly.

She turned on the light. It was a single large room, with low windows overlooking the street and a high ceiling that sloped up sharply. A small kitchen in one corner. An unmade bed in the opposite corner. Only the bathroom was closed off separately.

The walls were bare brick. The floor was bare wood. Several unframed paintings lay stacked against the walls. Lara went to the stereo, raised on plank-and-cinder-block shelves. She pushed the power button and stared at Jake, almost apprehensively.

The music was unlike anything he'd ever heard. In fact, there was no music, at least not in the sense of instruments. Just male voices singing in an austere choir.

"What is that?" Jake asked, cracking open the first beer and taking a grateful swallow.

"Gregorian chant," Lara said. "It's very old."

Jake nodded. *Okay*, he told himself, *so the girl has strange taste in music*. "Sounds like something Benjamin would like," he said.

Lara's eyes widened. "Really?" she asked eagerly.

Jake shrugged. "I guess. I mean, he listens to everything, but mostly he's into classical music."

"I knew he would be," Lara said mysteriously.

For lack of anything better to say, Jake offered her a beer. She took it and opened it with practiced ease, drinking off the first third in one swallow.

Lara took Jake's hand and walked him to the bed. She sat down, cross-legged despite the fact that she was wearing a skirt, and pulled Jake down beside her. She leaned forward, fixing him with her moist, intense eyes. "Tell me about the blind boy."

"Benjamin," Jake said.

"Yes. He says he's my half brother."

"Well, if Benjamin says it, I imagine it's true," Jake

said. He finished the first beer and got up to get them each a second.

"Maybe he only *believes* it's true," Lara said, smirking knowingly.

"I guess maybe it caught you by surprise, huh?" Jake said. "I mean, did you already know that you had this other father out there somewhere?"

"I knew the man who *pretended* to be my father wasn't," she said. "I asked my mother, and she told me it had been someone else. Only, she didn't tell me who."

"So I guess Benjamin was the one who spilled the beans."

"I knew before that. Benjamin doesn't know. He thinks he knows. But my real father isn't a *person* at all."

That stopped Jake in mid-swallow as alarm bells started going off in his head. He finished the second beer quickly and wondered whether he might not be able to find a better person to get drunk with on Halloween night. There must be parties going on all over the place.

On the other hand, this apartment was dry and warm, and he'd already carried the beer up four flights of stairs. And Lara might be a little loopy, but she was also quite pretty when you got beneath the bad makeup. The truth was, from certain angles she struck chords of memory in Jake, powerful, evocative memories of Zoey. When Lara smiled, especially, there was a clear flash of Zoey.

They were half sisters, after all, Jake reminded himself.

He cracked a third beer and handed one to Lara, who was keeping pace drink for drink. "So," Jake asked, knowing he really shouldn't, "who was your father?"

"Not who," Lara said. "*What.*"

Aisha reached the end of the alley and stepped out into the street. It was still rain slick, though the rain itself had stopped. Her head was feeling a little better. The throbbing was still there, but reduced to more support- able levels. The numbness on her side was almost all gone, just a hint of residual weakness remaining.

"I must look like a total mess," Aisha said to herself. "Jeff will think I'm a skank."

Her hair had suffered somewhat from being pressed down onto the ground. It was flatter on one side, with bits of grit stuck in it. Somehow, maybe because it was wet, it seemed slightly longer than should be right, too. First her uniform got all short and tight and now her hair had gone the other way, growing too long.

And where was her purse? Surely she wouldn't have left the house without her purse, with her brush and makeup. Had she left it back in the alley? No, she would have noticed it lying on the ground.

She started down the dark street, feeling a strange sort of anticipation, or was it nervousness? Not that she had anything to be nervous about. She was going to see Jeff. They would go up to his room and listen to music, and then his mother would go off to her night shift at the hospital. Jeff's mother left at eight, and Aisha had to be home by ten, her curfew, but that would still give them two hours of privacy together. At least it would if Jeff's aunts went out, too.

She thought of how much she enjoyed kissing Jeff. He was the only boy she had ever kissed, but just the same she was sure he was about the best kisser in the world. It was impossible to imagine anyone being sweeter, or more gentle, or more passionate.

He always told her how beautiful and sexy she was. And Aisha didn't need anyone to tell her how lucky *she* was that he liked her. He was older, after all, already seventeen years old, which was practically grown up.

Of course, him being older, he expected her to act more grown up than just some dumb fourteen-year-old.

Aisha thought about that as she turned onto Jeff's block. She wasn't stupid or anything; she knew what Jeff wanted her to do. Lots of girls at school were already doing it, and lots of them were doing it with dorky guys their own age. At least Jeff was older and more experienced. Not to mention so much more handsome.

And someday Jeff was going to be a big success with his music. He had already started performing on weekends in the T station downtown.

Aisha looked up, her attention drawn by a very unusual sight in this part of town: a limousine. It was black and glistened with raindrops and was coming toward her, slowly crawling along the street.

Aisha stopped to watch it go by. Possibly some major star was inside and she might be able to get a glimpse, although the windows were opaque.

The limousine stopped, and suddenly the door opened. To her complete and utter amazement, Jeff jumped out. He ran to her, crying out her name. He put his arms around her and twirled her around.

Aisha giggled. "Stop, you'll make me dizzy."

"Aisha," Jeff said happily. He held her out at arm's length, looking her over as if it had been a long time since he had seen her last, instead of just yesterday. "Damn, you look good, girl."

"I'm a mess," Aisha protested. "I think I tripped back in the alley. My uniform is soaked."

"Uniform?"

Aisha opened her coat. "See, it's wet all up one side."

"That your same old Girl Scout uniform?" Jeff asked, grinning delightedly. "Oh, I get it. Halloween. Well, this is my whole costume." He stepped back and spun around. He was dressed in hugely baggy jeans and a jean jacket with no shirt on underneath.

"Halloween?" Aisha asked, repeating the word uncomprehendingly.

"Not really," Jeff said with a self-deprecating look. "Just my stage rags. Now that I'm a big star I have to dress down."

"How come you're riding in that car?" Aisha asked, pointing at the limousine, as long as two normal cars.

"They sent it over for me from the Orpheum, baby. Like I say, now that I'm a big star I guess I rate a limo."

Aisha looked closely at him. He was acting very strange, and in fact he looked a little strange. Almost as if he was older. But that might have just been because she'd never seen him looking quite this happy. He couldn't stop smiling.

"So, me being an old friend and all, is it like cool if I give you a kiss?" he asked, smiling roguishly.

"You never asked before," Aisha pointed out.

Jeff took her in his arms and held her close. At first he gave her a light little kiss, just brushing her lips. Then he started to release her. Then he looked at her and must have seen her half-closed eyes and parted lips, because he came back again for a more normal kiss. They had been French-kissing for a few months already, and Aisha liked it a lot. It made her feel totally incredible.

Though as he kissed her, a strange thought crossed her mind. It was like a picture of some faraway place, a dark yard, and she herself in a bathrobe and a big green parka. Then the picture was gone and she was back, reveling in the way Jeff made her feel.

"Come on, baby," he said in a husky voice, pulling away at last. "I don't want to be late."

"Where are you going?" Aisha asked.

"Where are *we* going, you mean. Baby, we're on our way to the big time. The Orpheum."

"Why are we going there? What's going on?"

Jeff looked at her queerly for a moment. Then he laughed. "I see you picked up that dry Maine sense of humor."

"I did?"

"Okay, I get it," Jeff said. He laughed again. "Come on, hop in. This is it, babe. The first great gig. Opening for Salt-n-Pepa and Queen Latifah at the Orpheum."

"No way!" Aisha exclaimed. Then, more doubtful, "What is salt and pepper?"

Jeff sighed. "You never were big on music, I know, but come on. Even *you* must know who they are."

Aisha felt embarrassed. Obviously she was revealing her ignorance again, something she did frequently on the subject of music. "Of course I do," she said quickly. "I was just teasing."

She got in, shocked by the feel of the cold leather seats on her bare legs. She had to lean way out to close the door, but the driver had gotten out to close it for her. "Wow," Aisha said.

"You got that right," Jeff said. "Wow."

BENJAMIN

Well, I guess this is obvious, but my great fear is that somehow I'll lose my hearing. I'm already blind. I think being blind and deaf would be a little too much. No music. No conversation. No talking books. That would definitely be unpleasant. I might have to check out permanently at that point. I mean, what's left then? Taste? Smell? Touch?

I'll admit the sense of touch has some interesting possibilities. And with taste I could become a wine connoisseur and a serious gourmet. Which means a really hot Saturday night would be a delicious dinner, accompanied by an excellent wine while I enjoy the subtle hints of my girlfriend's perfume, and after dinner we give the sense of touch a workout . . .

Okay, so I guess I'm not afraid of anything. Unless you want to get into the whole "I'm-blind-so-any-passing-pinhead-can-beat-me-up" thing. Yeah. Well, all right, there is still this little bit of fear that someday someone, or several someones, will realize how defenseless I am. It's a world that still wants guys to be tough and able to protect themselves. And I'm not tough, not in that way at least. And I can't do much to defend myself. And yes, that does still scare me.

But I can put stuff like that out of my mind most of the time. The bigger fear, on a day-to-day basis, is just that I'll make some incredible fool of myself. It's taken a lot of work to earn people's respect, and boy, when you can't see, it is so easy to make an ass of yourself.

Fifteen

Benjamin moved forward cautiously because Nina was moving forward cautiously and because this was as far from familiar territory as he had been in a long time. Here there were no points of reference. Here he hadn't measured out distances, counting the number of steps, memorizing them. *Here* he was truly blind. Absolutely blind. If Nina decided for some reason to abandon him and walk away, he could wander for days or weeks or forever out here and never find his way to anything.

The only touchstone he had, aside from the reassuring contact with Nina, was the sweet sound of the violin. He could fix its direction: ahead and to the right. To some extent he could make an educated guess at the distance— perhaps a hundred yards now.

The other many things he heard, smelled, and felt added no clarity. His footsteps crunched on gravel and sandy soil and scattered pine needles. The air smelled of pine and mildew, decaying leaves and faint wood smoke. He heard water dripping down from branch to branch in the trees all around, plopping onto the forest floor. He heard the sound of Nina's breathing and his own. Both she and he, excited, breathing a little too fast. He knew his own heart was pounding and imagined that Nina's was as well.

"I see a light," Nina whispered. She stopped. Benjamin felt the muscle in her arm tighten.

"What kind of light?"

"I can't tell. It's yellowish. Looks like it's square, but I can only see it through the trees."

"Like a window?" Benjamin asked.

"Exactly like a window," Nina confirmed.

"That's good," Benjamin said, trying to exude confidence. "Where you have a window, you have a house. Where you have a house, you have a phone."

They started forward again, and in a few seconds Nina said, "Definitely a house. Wait! I see someone inside. He's . . . he's doing something, like swaying back and forth and moving his arms—"

"You mean like playing a violin?"

"Oh. Yeah. That's it. Duh."

"Duh," Benjamin agreed. "What's the house look like?"

"I can't see much, but I think it has a porch and it's wood."

"Okay. Forward."

They had gone a dozen steps when the loud barking erupted.

"A dog!" Nina yelled.

The violin music stopped instantly. Benjamin heard the barking coming at them. At any moment the dog would be on them, springing for his throat. The squeak of a door opening, then a rattling slam. A loud snarl, shockingly close.

"Hold, Moloch! Hold."

The voice was definitely not Nina's. It was harsh and male. Old, Benjamin decided, and then congratulated himself on being so analytical at a point when he was afraid his knees might buckle.

"What in hell are you doing on my land?"

"Um, we're like lost?" Nina said, falling into squeaky uptalk.

"Our van broke down," Benjamin added. "We were wondering if we could use your phone to call Triple A."

Silence. The dog still growled, only inches away, Benjamin was sure. Yes, within easy biting range.

"We heard your violin," Benjamin said helpfully.

"I wasn't playing it for you," the old man said.

Again silence. And now the rain began to fall again. Just a steady drizzle, not a downpour, but enough to quickly wet Benjamin's hair.

"Got no phone," the man said at last.

Benjamin could feel Nina's disappointment, transmitted through her arm.

"Better step inside," the man said, sounding doubtful and reluctant. Although no more reluctant than Benjamin. Still, the rain was falling harder now. There was a snarling dog at his feet. It was cold. They were lost. There weren't a lot of other options.

"That would be very kind of you," Benjamin said. *And if you don't murder us and feed us to your dog, that would be very kind, too*, he added silently.

Nina led him to steps. "Three," she said.

He climbed them and gratefully felt the moment when he passed under the shelter of the porch and the rain stopped falling on his head.

The sound of a rickety screen door opening on rusty hinges.

Nina shifted his grip and sidled through. It was warm, and from both the smell of smoke and the crackling sound, Benjamin knew there was a wood fire going.

"Blind, huh?"

"Yes, sir."

"Not too damned smart going for a walk in these woods when you can't even see."

Hard to argue with that, Benjamin admitted.

"Sit down," the old man said.

"Sharp right," Nina directed. "Two steps."

Benjamin followed the directions and found the chair. He sat down wearily. The fire's warmth could be felt not far away. Creaking floorboards, the sound of someone walking away.

"He stepped out of the room," Nina whispered. "By the way, don't make him mad. He's about ten feet tall."

"Ten feet?"

"Okay, about six inches taller than you, and big. He's old, but he looks all leathery and tough, you know?"

"Yeah, how big is the dog?" Benjamin whispered back.

"The dog? Oh, let's see: if you were standing and he was to walk right up and bite you, you'd be screaming in a soprano voice. Does that draw you a picture?"

"Wonderful. I could have lived without that particular picture."

"Here he comes."

"I made you each a cup of coffee. It's all I have. I don't do a lot of socializing. Not since the wife departed."

"Departed? Where did she go?" Benjamin heard Nina ask. He winced. Bad question.

"Departed this earth." The old man laughed, a dry, rasping sound. "She's burning in the everlasting fires of hell."

About ten seconds of absolute silence.

"Oh," Nina said.

"She hated it here. Couldn't stand the silence and loneliness," the old man said. "She wanted more. She wanted people around her. Excitement." He laughed the same harsh laugh. "So she got her excitement. Ayuh. She was excited, all right."

Another ten seconds of absolute silence.

"Well," Nina said brightly. "Thanks for the coffee.

If you don't have a phone, I guess we'll just head back to the van and wait for someone to drive by."

"You wouldn't like the sort of folks who might drive by on *this* night," the man said. "And you wouldn't half like the things you might see in these woods on a Halloween night."

Neither Nina nor Benjamin could think of a single thing to say in response to that.

"You'll sleep in the barn," the old man said with an air of absolute finality. "You'll keep warm and dry in there. Ol' Moloch will watch over you."

In the barn, Benjamin repeated. *Watched over by Moloch.* A dog named for an ancient god who was known to prefer human sacrifices.

Benjamin decided he probably should *not* mention that little fact to Nina.

"TV," Jeff said. "Check it out."

"Cool. I guess it can't get cable, though."

Jeff laughed. "Have to be a long cable."

He was showing her the features of the limo. The power window that went up, blocking off the driver. The refrigerator. The stereo.

They drove past the Granary Burying Ground in the limo and pulled up to the private back entrance to the Orpheum. It was beginning to dawn on Aisha that Jeff was telling the truth. She couldn't imagine how he had kept this from her, it was an awfully huge secret, but now it was starting to look as if it was true.

"I can't believe you didn't tell me about this. You sure can work a surprise."

"Now, Aisha, if I didn't tell you this was on, how is it you're here?" He looked at her with concern. "You didn't hurt yourself when you tripped in the alley, did you?"

Aisha didn't like his implication that she was being

weird or something. He was the one being weird. But this certainly wasn't the time to start a fight.

They were shown to a dressing room with a ragged leather couch, and Aisha waited there while Jeff went off to hook up with his DJ and the other guys and check out the stage. He asked her to come with him, but Aisha felt amazingly weary and said she wanted to take a little nap. That way she could be totally up when the show started.

"Yeah, I understand, Aisha," he said. "After that drive down here and all."

Aisha decided Jeff was a little distracted by all the excitement. He seemed to be saying things that made no sense at all. But given this sudden, amazing break in his career, his barely begun career, it wasn't surprising that he might get a little strange.

She'd intended just to rest a little, but waves of sleepiness reached up to her from the couch and drew her irresistibly. She couldn't remember ever being more tired.

Her sleep was confused and chaotic. Dreams melted one into the next. Images of a white man with a large nose and silver-gray hair. Images of Jeff, but a Jeff who kept turning into someone else, a smiling, handsome guy Aisha felt she must know; of a Girl Scout uniform that was too short; of spinning and falling; of a large boat, a ferry, approaching a small, quaint village.

She was standing in the dark, outside in a bathrobe and big, puffy coat, in front of a large house. Someone was approaching her, coming nearer in slow motion, his face hidden. But she wasn't frightened. On the contrary, she wanted the person to come closer, much closer. His name was . . . It was right there, on the tip of her tongue.

And then he was there, kissing her lips. It felt profoundly, deeply wonderful.

Aisha opened her eyes. Jeff pulled away, looking sheepish.

"Sorry," he said. "I couldn't help myself."

"I didn't mind at all," Aisha said shyly. "I was just dreaming about you." But as soon as she said it Aisha felt strange. Had she been dreaming about *Jeff*?

He leaned over her and kissed her again, and she forgot about her doubts.

"Missed you, baby," he said in a hoarse whisper.

Aisha felt his hand moving in a way that she had only recently begun to allow. Her mother would kill her if she knew she was letting him touch her this way, but it felt so good. "There's never been anyone like you for me," Jeff said in a whisper.

"I love you, Jeff," Aisha said.

His eyes widened in surprise. "You do? Still?"

"Of course, silly," Aisha said. "I only tell you every day."

"It's been a while," Jeff said.

Aisha frowned sternly. "Just yesterday."

"You're right," Jeff said with a smile. "It is just like yesterday."

There was a knock at the door. He rolled his eyes and yelled, "I'll be right there, stay out!" Then, in an intimate whisper, "It's getting close," he told Aisha, his eyes shining. "I can't believe this day. My biggest gig ever, and my number-one babe, right back here in my arms."

Aisha kissed him again. It was so cool that he really, really loved her. And she really, really loved him, too. "Maybe after the show something else lucky will happen," she said.

His eyes were smoldering. "Don't tease me."

She nodded slowly. "It's what I want," Aisha said, feeling suddenly very grown up and mature. It was something she'd been thinking about for a long time.

And what better night than this for it to happen? She was honored that he wanted her to be a part of all this.

"Are you sure?" Jeff asked. "Those are just the same words you used before. I don't know if you remember, but I do. Only this time, you know, I'll be totally careful." He made a cross-your-heart motion.

Again Aisha experienced that strange disconnection, the sense of confusion, of having not quite heard right or something. There was a second loud knock at the door. Someone yelled, "Five minutes, Mr. T-Bone!"

"Coming!" Jeff yelled. "Come on, baby," he said. "I want you out there with me. I don't want to take any chance that you'll suddenly disappear on me again."

"So where in the hell is she?" Christopher demanded for the thousandth time. They were standing in the crowd outside the Orpheum, a fairly unruly but not threatening bunch. The smell of pot smoke drifted by from time to time. Several competing boom boxes were blasting away just across the street in the Commons. A lone protester was parading around carrying a homemade sandwich board that denounced abortion, godlessness, the Trilateral Commission, the U.S. Postal Service, and Howard Stern.

At least Zoey *believed* he was a protester. It was hard to tell in a crowd of people, at least two thirds of whom were in costume. Zoey's own zombie cheerleader was among the tamer zombies, ghouls, and beasts, all breathing steam in the cold air. "This is the place, right?" Christopher demanded. He stood up on his toes and scanned the crowd as well as he could. "I mean, they open the doors in a few minutes and once we're inside, how's she going to find us? Man, I knew this was screwed somehow or other. I didn't know how exactly, but from the start it felt like some kind of mess about to happen."

"Christopher, Aisha's not the only one missing," Zoey pointed out. "While we're at it, where are Nina and Benjamin? Where's Claire? Okay, forget Claire, she did say she probably wouldn't come at all. But we are definitely missing three people."

"Beavis and Butt-head," Lucas remarked, pointing at a couple wearing the easily recognizable masks. "That makes three different B and B's so far. Two Barneys. And about two hundred gangsta-looking types who may, or may not, be in costume. And an awful lot of gorillas." He sighed. "I guess gorillas are fairly common, huh?"

"Maybe that's it," Zoey said. "Maybe we can't see them because they're in costume."

"Aisha was just wearing her old Girl Scout outfit, right?" Christopher argued. "I'd recognize that."

"There! That's like the eighth gorilla," Lucas said, outraged. "They're everywhere!"

"What are you worried about?" Zoey demanded. "You've barely put on your mask. And I have yet to see Christopher do his President Clinton, while here I am, walking around Boston wearing a pleated skirt, blue body makeup, and this dumb plastic cleaver on my head."

"I can't put on my mask," Christopher said. "I want Aisha to be able to spot me easily. I just don't see what could be keeping her so late." He looked at his watch yet again. "Damn."

"Look, Christopher," Zoey said impatiently, "Aisha is the last person we have to worry about. She grew up here. She knows her way around, unlike Nina and Benjamin. Aisha has friends here. Maybe she hooked up with some of them. Or maybe her old boyfriend—I, uh, I mean this guy T-Bone, Jeff, the guy who's playing, maybe she hooked up with him."

Zoey waited, hoping against hope that Christopher hadn't heard the word *boyfriend*. But Christopher had frozen in place. And now he was turning his suspicious glare on Zoey. "Boyfriend? Old boyfriend? This guy, this rapper, used to be her boyfriend? See, Aisha let that slip once before and then she went off telling me no, he *wasn't* ever her boyfriend."

"I didn't mean boyfriend like that," Zoey said quickly. "I meant he was a friend, and a boy, as opposed to a friend who's a girl."

But Christopher wasn't buying a word of it. "Boyfriend. I knew there was something going on here. Now I see it all clearly. That's why she wanted to come down to do this. And that's why she ditched us." He was pacing around in a tight circle and throwing his arms out every few words. "She's off with this dude right now, I guess. Talking about old times, huh? Yeah, I'll just bet they're *talking*."

"It's all ancient history," Zoey said placatingly. "Aisha was fourteen at the time. She doesn't even like to talk about him because it all ended badly. You know she loves you."

"She doesn't want to talk about it," Christopher said, "but here we all are to watch him, right? And where is *she* while we're out here?"

"Look, she asked you to come, Christopher," Zoey argued. "That should tell you something."

"She's probably backstage with him right now, him telling her how he's going to take her to Hollywood with him. Let her be in his music video, dancing around wearing those little shorts," Christopher said darkly. "And I'm out here worrying."

"Why don't we go on in?" Zoey suggested. "Maybe she's inside waiting for you."

But Christopher's face was all suspicion. "Maybe it might be interesting if I was to see her *before* she sees me," he said craftily. He slipped the Clinton mask on over his head. "Maybe I'll just go in and see what she's up to." He dug his ticket out of his pocket.

Lucas and Zoey exchanged a look. "Nina will take care of Benjamin," Zoey said with a shrug. "And vice versa. Whereas I think Christopher may be losing it."

"Hey, President Clinton," Lucas called after Christopher. "Wait up. The dead cheerleader and her gorilla are coming with you."

Sixteen

"I don't know if the blind boy is my true brother or not," Lara said. "Many things are not what they seem." She nodded in profound agreement with her own statement while Jake popped his seventh beer.

"Yep," Jake said indifferently. "Can't argue with that."

The first twelve-pack was finished. The red, white, and blue cans were stacked in a pyramid on a low, cigarette-burned coffee table. The second twelve-pack had been unwrapped, and Jake was gratified to see that he had begun to pull ahead of Lara. She had drunk him can for can until this seventh beer.

Not that she was acting drunk in any way. On the contrary, while Jake was getting more lighthearted and beginning to think that Lara was, after all, quite a pretty girl, and one who flopped around without the slightest seeming concern for modesty, Lara was growing ever more intense.

She had started several times to tell him her theory of who her father really was but had been interrupted by the need to fetch more beer from the refrigerator, the need to go to the bathroom, where she peed with the door open while singing along off-key with the chanting from the stereo. And once she had been interrupted by an apparent need to go to the window and shout obscenities at a car far below on the street that had blown its horn.

She was not an entirely normal girl.

Lara was sitting cross-legged now, halfway across the bed, leaning toward him with a serious expression. She pointed at him with her cigarette. The end glowed mesmerizingly, drawing unsteady circles in the dimly lit room. "No," she reiterated, "the blind boy may or may not be my brother. I don't know . . . *yet.* But what I do *know* is that the man he thinks is his father is not *my* father."

Jake stared at her stupidly for a few seconds. "How does that work out?"

She cocked her head sideways and looked at him appraisingly. She blew cigarette smoke toward him. He wondered what she would do if he tried to kiss her.

"I *know* who my real father was," Lara said, smiling mysteriously.

"Okay," Jake said patiently.

"I even know *what* he was."

"Yeah, you mentioned that before." Jake finished the seventh beer, upending the can.

"His name is Necrophage."

Jake nodded. "That sounds foreign."

Lara smiled mysteriously again, a smug, knowing expression that Jake realized vaguely would probably have annoyed him if he were sober. "Oh, it's foreign, all right."

"Greek? Sounds like it might be Greek. Is your real father Greek?" In about ten seconds he was going to make his move. What was the worst she could do? Slap him?

"He's a demon," Lara said.

"My dad's like that sometimes," Jake said.

"No!" Lara nearly shouted. Her eyes blazed angrily.

She puffed several times dramatically on her cigarette. "Don't act like I'm crazy or something. He's a demon. I'm not saying he's Satan *himself* or anything. *That* would be crazy."

Jake had been within seconds of reaching for her exposed, accessible leg. He looked sharply at her. "Huh?"

"My father is the demon Necrophage," Lara said, managing to sound almost proud.

"A demon. As in from hell?"

"He can be in hell any time he wants," Lara said, "but he walks the earth. Only in bed does he reveal himself as a demon. The only thing I can't figure out is the blind boy."

Jake was sobering up slightly. "That's *all* you can't figure out?" he asked cautiously. Maybe she was just drunk and free-associating and a little unusual. Or maybe she was insane. Really, truly insane.

"I don't know if the blind boy is a son of Necrophage or not," Lara said. "The blindness may be a sign."

Jake actually smiled. The image of Benjamin hearing that he was the son of a demon named Necrophage was definitely amusing. "I guess I could ask him, next time I see him," Jake offered.

"We can find out right now," Lara said.

"Oh, really?"

She jumped up suddenly and ran to one of the plank-and-cinder-block shelves. She came back with a rectangular brown board and a heart-shaped piece of plastic. "Have you ever consulted a Ouija board before?" Lara asked. She set the board reverently between them on the bed, carefully positioning the plastic shuttle.

"I, uh . . . no." More beer would be needed for this.

"Just place your fingers very lightly, like this," Lara instructed.

"You know, Lara, it's getting kind of late," Jake said.

She looked at him appraisingly for a minute, staring

straight into his eyes in a way that made him want to flinch. "I'll call on my spirit," she said at last. "And after I learn about the blind boy I'll ask her whether I should give you my body." She grinned slyly, knowingly. "You do think I'm that other girl's half sister, don't you? That's why you look at me like that."

Jake fought to keep his expression calm. It was the second time that night that Lara had seemed to reach into his mind and extract information she shouldn't have known. How had Lara guessed that when he looked into her burning, intense blue eyes he was looking for echoes of Zoey?

The same way she had known that Wade's license picture was of a dead person?

Without a word Jake put his fingers on the shuttle. The CD reached its last few notes and died away, leaving silence behind. The atmosphere seemed to have grown thick and stifling. Just the cigarette smoke, Jake reassured himself. And this sense of strangeness, of things creeping around him unseen, that was just the beer. He made a mental note: in future, don't drink with lunatics.

"Look into my eyes and concentrate," Lara ordered.

Jake did. Their eyes met, and it was as if an electric connection had been made. Her eyes captivated him, held him. Like Zoey's? Yes. The same blue. The same shape. But what was behind them was different. Very different.

"Are you with us, O spirit?" Lara asked the smoke-laced air.

For a long while they waited, barely breathing. Fingers trembling on the edge of the shuttle.

"Are you with us, O spirit?" Lara asked again.

Suddenly, to Jake's amazement, the shuttle moved. It slid in a shallow arc across the board and came to rest pointing at the word *Yes*.

Drunk or not, Jake was beginning to feel very nervous. He glanced over his shoulder toward the dark corner of the room. They were alone, he reassured himself. Lara might be crazy, but he was twice her size. There was nothing for him to fear.

"It feels different," Lara said, creasing her brow. "Is this Amber?" In an aside she explained, "Amber is my spirit guide. Amber Shores. She was killed by Indians in 1649."

Despite himself Jake felt a crawling sensation on his skin. Sweat was trickling down his back. His fingers were twitching from the effort it took to hold them still.

"Is this Amber?" Lara repeated the question.

The shuttle moved quite strongly to *No*.

Lara's eyes opened wide in surprise. "Then please tell us your name, O spirit."

The shuttle moved slowly, uncertainly around the board, wandering, as if it was learning its way around. It stopped, pointing at *W*.

"Go on," Lara urged. "We wish to speak to you, O spirit from beyond the grave."

The shuttle moved to the *A*.

Jake stopped breathing. He could swear *he* wasn't moving the shuttle.

"*W* and *A*," Lara whispered. "Remember that."

The shuttle moved, strongly this time. *D*.

Jake felt his heart miss several beats. The hairs on the back of his neck were on end. He wasn't going to let the shuttle move. He wasn't going to let it show the next letter. He wasn't going to let it move to *E*.

"You're fighting it," Lara said accusingly.

"No," Jake said. The shuttle moved. Despite his every effort to hold his hands still, the shuttle moved. Inch by inch across the board.

"Spell out your name, O spirit from beyond the grave!" Lara cried in a transport of enthusiasm.

Jake stared in horror as the pointer moved vindictively, irresistibly to the *E*.

"W-A-D-E," Lara said. "I wonder if there's more?"

Jake stood up and backed away. He tripped over his feet and fell down but was up in a flash.

"Don't be scared, Jake," Lara said. "It's just a spirit. The dead can't hurt us."

But Jake was past hearing.

"Are you hungry?" Sean asked.

"No," Claire said. "I don't seem to be interested in food." He smiled. "I'll take that as a sign that you aren't bored with me just yet."

No, she wasn't bored. Very far from it. She was interested in everything about him.

They had talked and talked for what seemed like hours. In the time that Claire and Sean had been sitting in the airport restaurant, drinking cup after cup of coffee, they had talked more than they had in all their computer conversations.

She had gotten used to his odd, slight hesitancy every time he spoke. The way he seemed to be searching for the right thing to say, and inevitably finding it.

She sat now with her chin resting on her hand, feeling like she had never felt before. Feeling like some great power of the universe had given her exactly what she had been looking for. Looking for, without ever consciously knowing it.

Sean was brilliant, and witty, and had flashing perfect teeth. He was sexy, without being pushy or crude. Funny, but not condescending. Handsome, but modest. He laughed at her jokes. He remembered everything she had ever told him about herself.

He had thought about her, considered her as a person. Yes, he knew her weaknesses, but he also knew her strengths. He was forgiving and kind, and still had flashing perfect teeth.

She had liked him as an abstraction when he had just been a line of type on the computer screen. She had thought even then that he was uncommonly smart and thoughtful. But in person the effect was overwhelming. And Claire wasn't a person who had ever been overwhelmed by anyone or anything.

He was in every way perfect. And he had no girlfriend. And he liked her very much. And Claire's usual cool reserve was being swamped by her growing desire to touch him, to kiss him.

"I know it's a cliché about flying that it makes you feel free, but I can't help the facts: it *does* make you feel free. It *is* exhilarating."

"So, how long before you can fly a passenger jet like your dad?"

The hesitation. The flash of teeth. "A very long time. Right now I can only fly myself and whatever fool will volunteer to fly with me."

"I'll fly with you," Claire said, sounding ridiculously sultry to her own ears.

Sean's eyes flew open in alarm. Beyond him Claire saw the fat guy, still reading his book, smile wickedly. Then the smile evaporated, and he looked back down at his book, mumbling the words to himself.

"That's awfully nice of you to show such confidence in my flying," Sean said, "however misplaced." He grinned self-deprecatingly. He reached across the table and for the first time took her hand in his. "But on a rainy night like this, I wouldn't want to endanger a person I care a great deal about."

Claire was aware—very aware—of a physical response to his touch. Of a warmth that made her squirm a little in her chair. She blushed again, practically making a habit of it. "Too bad we have to hang around here," she said.

"Who says we have to?" Sean said in a low voice. He flushed and put his hand to his hearing aid. Then he said, "You know those Z-iosks? They have them all around the airport, and it's like this little room, you know? With a chair and table and like this bed? I guess people like sleep in them while they're stuck waiting."

"I've seen them," Claire admitted. The word *bed* had brought her up short. Apparently it had disturbed Sean as well. He was stammering and flushing and not sounding at all like himself. Still, Claire reflected, some privacy would be nice. She badly wanted Sean to kiss her. Probably more than once. Probably in a way that he couldn't do out here in a restaurant.

"All you need is a credit card," Sean said. "Do you have one?"

"Sure," Claire said.

"Then let's go, okay?"

She considered for a moment. Saying yes would make it so obvious that she wanted to kiss him. It would mean surrendering all her power over the situation.

Saying no would be worse.

"I've never seen inside a Z-iosk," she said.

Sean got up quickly, threw some money down on the table, and took Claire's arm. He hustled her away with surprising force, almost enough to make her resentful. He led the way to the Z-iosk. It looked from the outside like a cross between a tiny trailer and an oversize, old-fashioned phone booth.

Claire extracted her Visa card and stuck it in the slot. The door opened, and inside she saw a narrow, built-in cot on one side, a chair, a TV set high on the wall, and a table.

"Perfect," Sean said, rubbing his hands together.

Claire wasn't so sure. With the door closed behind

them and the blinds on the door drawn shut, it was completely private. Completely. She wanted to kiss him, yes. But it would be awkward if he thought she was ready for more.

Quite suddenly Sean took her in his arms and kissed her lips. It was a surprise, but oh, not a bad one. After a moment's hesitation Claire returned the kiss. And after a moment's more hesitation she let Sean draw her down onto the bed.

Claire

What am I frightened of? Severe, third-degree burns. Paralysis from the neck down. I could live without either of those. I'm not fond of pain and helplessness.

Also, I guess I'd rather not end up completely alone. Mostly alone would be great, but not completely. I suppose I would be happy if I had just one good friend. And one real boyfriend, a guy who loved me for what I am. Or despite what I am. And yet it's all too easy for me to envision a future where I don't manage even that much. I don't worry about school, or money, or success. Those things are all easy for me. It's just the little human things I have problems with: trust, love. Those things.

I can see me ten or twenty years from now. A success, of course. Respected. Admired. Desired.

A lone.

I guess it sounds pathetic and maudlin, but I'm afraid that there is just something about me that will never let me be truly loved. But I'm not going to change just to make people love me. I make people take me as I am. Or they can forget it.

What I'm afraid of is that they might just decide, given those options, to forget it.

Seventeen

The old man and the dog together led Nina and Benjamin to the barn. He pointed to fresh straw they could sleep on. He pointed to the cow and advised them to stay away from her. He showed them the water pump. Then he left them.

"He's gone," Nina whispered.

"How about the dog?" Benjamin whispered back.

"Him too."

The two of them breathed a sigh of relief.

Nina looked around at their surroundings. A single lightbulb, swinging lazily from the roof on a long cord, provided light. "It seems we have a cow," Nina said. "She's in a stall. There are like three other stalls, but they're all empty. There's an upstairs."

"A loft?"

"Okay," Nina said, "sure, I guess that's a loft. I've never seen a loft before. It's like half an upstairs, you know what I mean?"

"Yeah, it's called a loft," Benjamin said.

The cow stuck its head over the railing of its stall and glared at them with a single, huge brown eye. Then it mooed, an amazingly loud sound.

"Damn!" Benjamin said.

"That was the cow," Nina said quickly, putting a hand over her fluttering heart.

"Really?" Benjamin grinned. "You're telling me the cow goes moo?"

"You know, you're getting sarcastic, Benjamin," Nina warned.

"I have mud *inside* my pants," Benjamin said. "If all I get is sarcastic, it will be a miracle."

"There's water over there," Nina said. "You could wash off. You could change into your costume while your regular clothes dry. See, I told you it was a good idea to bring the costumes. Ha!"

Benjamin considered for a moment. "I know this is a silly question, but you don't really think Farmer Joe here is a mad killer who will reappear in a few minutes wearing a hockey mask and swinging a machete, do you?"

"What makes you think that?" Nina asked, trying unsuccessfully to sound nonchalant.

"Oh, maybe it was the remark about his wife burning in hell. Maybe that's what set off my suspicions."

"There's that sarcasm again."

"Or it could have been all that stuff about not liking what we'd see in these woods on a Halloween night. You have to admit, that sounds an awful lot like something a guy in a horror movie would say, right before he gets ready to hack everyone up with a machete."

"I was telling myself maybe he's just a lonely old guy whose wife died."

"Died? You don't think he killed her?"

"I was thinking like she ran off with someone exciting, like some kind of rock star or TV executive or something," Nina said thoughtfully. "Ran off and left the old man here all alone and bitter. Then it turned out that she died in an earthquake out in Los Angeles, and even though the old guy hated her for leaving, he was still destroyed over her death and it drove him nuts."

Benjamin waited. "Are you done?"

"Yeah, that's it," Nina said.

"My question is: Should we try to get back to the van or stay here?"

"If he's a mad slasher, he can get us here or there, and here it's nice and warm and we have light. Also," she pointed out, seizing on the idea, "here we have a pitchfork for self-defense."

"We do?"

"Yep." Nina went and lifted the pitchfork from where it was leaning against the wall. She handed it to Benjamin, who ran his hands over it thoughtfully.

"Okay, point me to the water. I'll wash off this mud. If I'm going to be hacked up by a madman, I'd like to be clean."

Nina led him across the barn to an old-fashioned-looking water pump in one corner. It spilled into a long wooden trough that was half-filled with water. A greenish scum had formed over the surface. Nina worked the handle a few times, using all her strength, and after several pumps the water splashed out clear and clean.

"Just use the water from the pump and stay out of the trough," Nina advised. "The backpack is right here." She dropped it beside him.

"Okay," Benjamin said. "Um, where are you going to be?"

"Oh." Nina looked around. "I'll go up to the loft and lay out our beds of nice, clean straw. Maybe later the Wise Men will come by with some frankincense."

"Okay," Benjamin said uncomfortably. "You're not going to be immature and look, are you?"

"I'm not that tacky," Nina said haughtily. "Your secrets are safe with me. Like I'd even be interested."

She turned her back and began climbing up the ladder to the loft. Up there, with the rafters just over her head and clean hay stacked in neat bales, it was a more pleasant, reassuring place. Armed with a pitchfork they'd be fine.

"It's nice up here!" Nina yelled down. There was no answer. Nina went to the edge of the loft and looked down. What she saw made her catch her breath. Benjamin was bent over, rinsing his clothing under the stream of water, his bare flesh lit by the single overhead light.

Nina pulled back and drew several deep breaths. Tacky. Tacky and sleazy and dishonest and not very nice, she told herself. Not that she had looked on purpose.

Of course, when she crept silently back to the edge of the loft and looked again, it *was* on purpose. Benjamin was pulling on his costume, muttering to himself as he got his foot stuck in an armhole.

"I'm putting on a red satin tuxedo, dressing up as Satan, in a barn in the middle of nowhere, with no one around but a nutty old man and a dog named Moloch," he said, pitching his voice loud so she could hear. "I'm telling you, there are elements of a Stephen King story here. And I don't like it."

Suddenly, from an indeterminate distance, a shriek broke the silence. It rose, a desperate, horrible wail, and fell, and rose again, louder than ever.

The dog started barking ferociously somewhere outside, howling and baying as if in answer to the terrifying wail.

"Nina!"

"Benjamin!"

"What was that?"

It came again. It was fairly far off, Nina decided, but not far enough. Not nearly far enough.

Nina began clambering down from the loft, shaking so badly that she missed several rungs in the ladder. She fell and rolled over, then bounded to her feet. Benjamin felt for the pitchfork, frantically pulling on the rest of his costume.

"What was that?" Nina cried.

"I don't want to know!" Benjamin yelled.

"Let's get out of here before he comes after us!"

"I'll stab this pitchfork right into that damned dog if he comes after us!" Benjamin threatened.

Nina grabbed his free hand and raced for the big, swinging door. To her relief it opened. Ha! The farmer had forgotten to lock them into his little trap.

"Let's run for it!" Nina yelled. Benjamin grabbed her arm and together they raced across the yard in front of the house, running in blind terror, followed by the frenzied howls of Moloch.

Aisha stood off to the side of the stage, feeling silly and conspicuous and far too young to be cool, especially in her dorky Girl Scout uniform. It was really time to quit Scouts, she told herself. Now she was actually glad the uniform had mysteriously shrunk. It at least made her look slightly sexy, and it was Halloween after all, so maybe people would just think it was a costume or something.

Halloween? How had it come to be Halloween?

The backstage area was filled with people, all of whom looked terribly busy and kept jostling her aside to run off on one last-minute errand or another. Jeff was onstage with his group, checking the amps and making last-minute changes in the program. The curtain was still down, but Aisha had heard an old man with a microphone headpiece yell to Jeff, "One minute to curtain!"

From beyond the curtain came a huge, restless noise. More than a thousand rowdy, yelling, singing, impatient voices. Most were chanting rhythmically now for the show to begin.

Jeff checked his mike for the hundredth time and

wiped his palms several times on his pants. He rolled his head around on his shoulders, trying to ease the tension. Then he looked over at her and smiled. A smile that said, Wow, can you believe this?

Aisha smiled back.

The curtain parted. Brilliant lights hit the stage, turning Jeff's familiar face blue. The crowd exploded in sustained applause and shouts. They would make more noise later for the well-known acts, Aisha knew, but she could see the way Jeff soaked up the waves of approval that washed over the stage.

He took a deep breath.

"About time," Christopher grumbled from beneath his President Clinton mask. "They're five minutes late. Okay, do you guys see Aisha anywhere?"

"I don't see Aisha, or Nina, or Benjamin!" Zoey said in frustration, yelling to be heard over the music. She was hemmed on every side by weirdly costumed, heaving, hand-waving, dancing bodies.

"They could be ten feet away in here and we wouldn't see them!" Lucas yelled. "Should have stayed back in our seats, not come down here to the mosh pit."

"If Aisha's here at all, she'll be down here, kissing up to her famous *former, ex, used-to-be* boyfriend!" Christopher said, yelling twice as loud to be heard through the rubber mask and still convey the heavy sarcasm. "She'll be down here dancing around where he'd notice her, no doubt. So *that's* the guy, huh?"

Zoey saw he was pointing at the lead rapper, a handsome guy with quite an excellent build. She remembered him from a picture Aisha had shown her, after she'd blurted the truth to her and Nina. He didn't look as if he'd changed much, if at all. "I don't know if that's him," she lied.

"I'll bet it is," Christopher said. "What, is he like hotter looking than me or something?"

Lucas put his hand on Christopher's shoulder. "Christopher, you know I've always thought you were the hottest looking."

The joke didn't mollify Christopher. He continued peering through the eye slits of the mask, trying to see past the blinding spotlights into the gloom of the backstage. "I wonder if I could get back there."

"They have bouncers, man, get a grip," Lucas said. "You'll get your ass kicked."

The first rap ended in a flurry of verbal agility and the room erupted in applause.

Up on the stage, Jeff knew. He could feel the quality of the applause. This was no longer polite applause. It was no longer "Hey, brother, we'll listen to your rap and give you a chance" applause. This was different. They had *loved* it. He had killed. They were smiling up at him now, those who weren't wearing masks. Smiling up at him and waiting for his next number.

Ah, so sweet. He raised his arms to take in the applause. Not too much, didn't want to look like he was getting too into it, but damn! The applause!

He caught sight of a figure out of the corner of his eye. Aisha standing in the wings and applauding wildly. Standing there in her silly Scout uniform, she looked so much like the girl he had loved three years before. Unchanged, almost, except that now she was taller, and her hair had grown out a little more. Still beautiful. Still so sexy. And after the performance here, he would give her another performance back in the dressing room. They would do the wild thing together, just like the good old days. And after that, pack her back off to Maine and, well . . . he looked down and saw an especially pretty girl, with an exceptionally nice body, who was most definitely giving him the eye ... well, now that he was a success, the opportunities were so plentiful.

Aisha applauded till her hands hurt. Jeff launched into the opening riff of his next rap, bounding around the stage with a degree of confidence she'd never seen before. It was amazing. It was like he had acquired years of experience overnight. Maybe that's what having a huge audience did for a performer. And these raps, she'd never heard either of them before and both were so much more sophisticated.

Not that she knew much about music, she reminded herself. She wasn't like Nina or Benjamin, obsessed by it.

Aisha froze. *Nina? Benjamin?* Where had those names come from? She didn't know anyone named Nina or Benjamin.

Did she?

She searched her mind, but her head had started spinning. Images flashed before her eyes. An alleyway. Two figures coming toward her, a gorilla. Yes, one was a gorilla. No, a man in a gorilla mask. And the other? A white man with a big nose and silver hair. Something familiar about the white man. Like she knew him from somewhere. Unconsciously Aisha put her hand to her head. She could feel the lump where her head had struck when she'd tripped in the alley.

Tripped? Had she tripped, or—

Applause again, louder than before as Jeff finished his second number. And now he was suddenly emerging from the brilliant spotlights, coming toward her, smiling hugely and catching her up around the waist.

He kissed her at the edge of the spotlight. Kissed her in sheer joy and exuberance. "I'm so glad you're here, baby," he said in her ear.

*   *   *

"SON OF A BITCH!" Christopher cried from beneath his Clinton mask.

"Oh, my God," Zoey said a little more quietly.

"Whoa, Aisha," Lucas said, an astonished gorilla.

"Look!" Christopher cried, pointing unnecessarily.

"I saw," Zoey said. She nodded, and the plastic cleaver slipped off her head.

"I think everybody saw," Lucas pointed out mildly.

"He kissed her!"

"Well . . ."

"He kissed her on the mouth. And there was tongue!"

"You can't be sure there was tongue!" Zoey said, shouting again over the renewed music as Jeff started his third and final number.

"There was tongue!" Christopher howled.

"Look, they're old friends," Zoey said. "They used to go together. Maybe she was just caught up in the excitement of the moment."

"Excitement of the moment?" Christopher bayed. He pulled Zoey close, yelling in her ear. "That 'old friends, used to go together' bull may be okay for you, Zoey, but not for me. Just because you don't care if Lucas sticks his tongue down Claire's throat in the front seat of her daddy's Mercedes does *not* mean it's okay with me for Aisha to be Frenching some sleazy *pimple* in front of a thousand people."

It took several long, slow seconds for what Christopher had said to begin to sink into Zoey's consciousness.

Christopher tore off through the crowd, making his way to the stage, an angry, determined President Clinton. A gorilla chased behind him, shouting that the bouncers would kill him.

Eighteen

"Mmm," Claire said.

"Yes," Sean breathed. "Definitely, mmm."

It was a very good kiss, Claire decided. As was the next one, and the one after that. Sean was definitely an overwhelming physical presence. She felt hard, lean muscle beneath his shirt. Strong, corded arms wrapped around her. It was one of the sensual pleasures she had always appreciated in Jake. And Sean was like some perfect combination of Jake's powerful physique and Benjamin's intelligence and even Lucas's tough sweetness.

"I think we'd better do that again, sweet thing," Sean said.

She was lying half-atop him on the bed, her black silken hair falling down around his shoulders and neck. He put his hand behind her head and drew her lips down to his again. Yes, he could kiss.

Claire heard a strange tinny sound, like a tiny radio far off. A voice yelling.

"What's that?" she asked.

Sean looked startled. Then his eyes narrowed craftily. "Oh, *that*. Just my hearing aid. Sometimes it picks up radio, believe it or not." He removed the device and fumbled at a minuscule switch. Claire heard the voice more clearly now, though not enough to make out the words. Then it went silent. Sean laid it on the table and pulled what must have been the battery pack or something, a rectangular object as small as the smallest tape player, out of an inner pocket. He tossed all this on the table.

"Now, babe, it's just you and me," he said, leering up at her. His hand went with practiced confidence to the buttons of her blouse. At the same time, with his other hand he pulled her down for another kiss.

It was still a wonderful kiss. But something had gone wrong. Claire felt it: a nagging feeling, deeply submerged in her consciousness. Deeply submerged but rising.

He was touching her now, expertly, wonderfully. "Damn, you are a hot bitch," he said.

Damn, you are a hot bitch? Claire reran the phrase in her mind. And the earlier *Now, babe, it's just you and me.*

His lips followed the line of her throat down, down. She shuddered and felt her body respond, even as her mind, her ever-cool, too-detached, too-reasonable mind worked at the problem. She had communicated with Sean via computer for many hours. She had now talked to him face-to-face for several more hours. There were few people with whom she had talked as much in one way or another. And she knew the way Sean talked. Knew his choice of words.

His lips drew an involuntary moan from her. "Oh, you like that, don't you?" Sean said in a whisper. "Just remember, babe, don't scream too much when we get to the good stuff. These walls are thin."

No, Claire told herself. *Don't. Don't let your suspicious mind do this. Don't spoil this wonderful moment with this perfect, transcendently wonderful guy, this guy*

*who likes you . . . maybe even loves you . . . despite all
he knows about you.*

I can put it out of my mind, Claire told herself firmly.
*I can ignore the doubt. I can just enjoy . . . I can just let
myself go . . . I can just—*

No. No, she realized ruefully, in the end she couldn't.
She pushed away, rolled off Sean, and stood up.

"What's the problem?" he asked. "Not getting cold
feet, are you? Is it the rubber thing? Because I have
condoms with me, sweet thing, never you worry."

Claire buttoned her blouse and looked down disgust-
edly at him. "Damn. I was almost going to buy it," she
admitted. "I mean, I knew something was off, but I
guess I didn't want to accept it."

"What are you talking about?" He flashed a quizzical
smile. A smile full of perfect teeth.

Claire sighed heavily. "What is your name, really?"

"Sean," he said. But doubt and worry were there in
his eyes, too.

Claire laughed. "No. Afraid not, although I sure
wanted you to be."

"What do you care who I am?" he asked. "You see
something here you don't like?"

"Yeah. I see a lot of teeth and no brain. And by the
way, whoever you are, I may be a bitch, but anyone who
knows me could tell you: I'm not a *hot* one."

Aisha retreated from the edge of the spotlight, but
even as she sidled gratefully back into obscurity, she saw
a strange figure shoving his way through the crowd below the stage, a person in a mask—a mask that tugged
at chords of memory. And then she could almost swear
someone had yelled out her name, though in all the
noise, that seemed unlikely. And yet the person in the
mask was waving his arms at her. And now she was
certain he was pointing at her, almost angrily. Suddenly

another person emerged from the crowd. This person wore a gorilla mask.

Aisha reeled. An alleyway. Two people coming toward her. One was wearing a gorilla mask and the other ... this same, unfamiliar mask of a white man with silver-gray hair.

They had grabbed her purse and pushed her! Now she remembered. And she had fallen. She remembered the solid impact of her head against the brick wall.

The one in the President Clinton mask was trying to climb the stage now. . . .

President Clinton? What was she thinking about? The president was Bush, wasn't he?

Aisha shook her head, trying to clear away a deluge of strange flashes, familiar images, and other images that seemed familiar but couldn't possibly be.

Aisha turned away in panic and confusion and ran, stumbling back toward the dressing room. From behind her, applause erupted, loud and sustained. She found the dressing room and closed the door. She leaned against it, panting in the dark.

"Am I going nuts, or what?" she asked the empty room. Yes, maybe that *was* it. Maybe she *was* going crazy.

Something was in her head, twisting her thoughts, and suddenly Aisha realized that she was very afraid.

The security guards caught him halfway up the side of the stage.

"Let me go, man, I'm cool!" Christopher yelled. He got a hand free and tore off his mask. "I'm cool, I'm cool. I just wanted to talk to the lady."

"Let him go," one guard told the other. "Can't go onstage, man," he instructed Christopher.

"He knows that, he understands," Lucas said, removing his own mask. "Jeez, Christopher, get a grip."

The zombie cheerleader finally made her way through the crowd and caught up with them. Zoey gave Lucas a cold, deadly look. Lucas had been holding on to a faint hope that somehow, in all the noise, Zoey hadn't heard Christopher stupidly blurting out what he should *not* have blurted. Her look put an end to that hope.

Amid all the noise Lucas felt a terrible, empty quiet settling around him, as if he had been cut off from all sensation. He should have known that sooner or later the truth would come out. Maybe he *had* known it.

"Oh, God," Lucas murmured. He looked pleadingly at Zoey, but she turned stonily away, focusing on Christopher.

"Are you okay, Christopher?" Zoey asked.

"I'm cool," he said. The first band had left the stage and now, waiting for the main acts, the audience had taken up a raucous chant.

Zoey nodded. "Lucas, I need to talk to you." She walked away several feet, finding what privacy there was in a relatively quiet corner, still hemmed in by bodies, but at least not crushed.

"Lucas, what did Christopher mean about you making out with Claire in the front seat of her dad's car?"

"Zoey, look . . ." Lucas tried desperately.

But Zoey had already seen the truth in his eyes. She shook her head bitterly. "Aren't you clever?" she snapped. "So you didn't *sleep* with Claire. You just made out with her. And I spend all week apologizing like I was a jerk for believing Jake."

"We didn't do anything but kiss a little," Lucas said lamely.

"You bastard."

"Zoey," Lucas pleaded, "it was nothing. We were both mad. Claire was mad at Jake, and I was mad at you. I thought you were getting ready to dump me and go back to Jake."

"You and Claire," Zoey said bitterly. "My mother screwing Mr. McRoyan, you trying to screw Claire, and look, even Aisha now. God, it's sickening. Is everyone just that way? Is everyone on earth just ready to stab anyone in the back?"

"Zoey, look, sometimes people make mistakes. I made one with Claire. I'm sorry. I knew even then it was a mistake."

"Right after she said no, right?" Zoey demanded cynically. "Then you thought, 'gee, I guess this is a big mistake.' "

"Zoey, I love you," Lucas said. "I'm sorry!" He had to shout because Salt-n-Pepa had come onstage to thunderous applause.

"Let me ask you something, Lucas," Zoey snapped furiously. "What button were you undoing at the moment you decided you were making a mistake? Or was it a bra hook? Or was it a zipper?"

Lucas was shocked at the force of her attack. But what could he say? Don't lump me in with what's going on between your mom and dad? Don't punish me for what you're feeling about them?

"I'm going home," Zoey said coldly. "I don't know if I can catch a train, or a bus, or maybe I'll rent a car; I don't give a damn as long as I'm not with you anymore."

He grabbed her arm. "Zoey," he pleaded, "you have to forgive me. You're . . . You're all I have."

For a moment it looked as if she might soften. But then her eyes went opaque, and she shook off his arm. "I guess you should have thought of that."

"Please, Lord, help me," Aisha begged, clasping her hands tightly together.

She had left the lights in the room off, an attempt to help soothe her headache. The headache had in fact less-

158

ened, but the confusion had not. Her brain was swimming with faces and places she half-knew, but knew she couldn't *really* know: a pretty girl with blond hair and blue eyes, a yellow and red and white ferry, a blind boy with an infectiously amused smirk, a big house with dozens of windows.

And mostly a guy who looked sort of like Jeff, only different.

She was losing her mind. Going insane, and this was the way it felt—all confusion and fear.

The door of the dressing room flew open. "Damn, we kicked out there!" Jeff said enthusiastically. He came running over to her and sat down, almost vibrating with excitement. "Did you hear the crowd? I mean, amazing. They were yelling out 'T-bone, T-bone' like it was some big thing, you know? Like . . . Like, I don't know."

"You were great," Aisha managed to say, trying to rise out of her mental confusion, feeling relieved just to have him near. She couldn't go insane as long as Jeff was there with her. He would keep her grounded.

"I mean, I thought it might be good," he said, "but I wouldn't let myself even start to think it would be this great. I'm on the way now. I'm on the road. People have to listen to us now, Eesh. I wouldn't be surprised if I'm talking record contract within like a week or two."

Aisha forced a smile and seized his arm tightly, holding on for dear life. "I am so proud of you," she said, chattering, talking to drive the voices of lunacy out of her mind. "I can't believe this all happened so suddenly. I didn't even know."

"It has been three years," he said. "I don't know if that's sudden."

"Three years?" Aisha said bleakly. "Don't do that, Jeff. I mean, it's only been a few weeks. Okay?"

"I guess it does *seem* like it hasn't been all that long to you, baby, but to me it feels like it's been a long time

159

in coming." He turned more to face her. She clung to him. "Let's celebrate the whole night."

"I . . . I don't know if my mom will let me stay out all night," Aisha said. Her mother. Home in Maine. Maine? Boston? Where did she live?

Jeff laughed, as if she'd told a joke. "What she doesn't know won't hurt her," he said. Then, in a lower voice, "And what I'm going to do won't hurt you either."

Aisha felt a little sick, but whether it was from the terrible, swirling voices in her head or the thought of what Jeff wanted to do now, she wasn't sure. Both, maybe. She had told him she would, but now it was the last thing she was interested in. She was losing her mind! She could feel it.

Jeff kissed her, and that cleared some of the confusion away. His closeness helped her focus. She knew where she was. She was with Jeff. *This* was real. The feel of his lips as he kissed her again, more urgently, passionately. Yes, *this* was real.

His hands were moving over her body, faster, more confidently than he had ever done before. No hesitation. So direct! He was moving over her, laying her down on the couch before she had any time to think or object. And mostly she didn't *want* to object. She wanted to do this if only to hold on to the one stable image in her brain.

Yes, that was the answer. Just do it quickly. With her eyes closed and Jeff in her arms, the other images faded and the strange voices quieted.

But even now another voice reminded her. She smiled to herself. This voice at least wasn't part of the insanity. "Jeff, don't forget to use a thingy," she whispered in his ear.

"We don't need to worry about that," he said.

"Christopher," Aisha said, mustering more determination, "that's what you said last time."

"*Christopher?* What did you call me? Christopher?"

Last time? Aisha reran the phrase in her mind. *That's what you said last time?* What had she been thinking of? What last time? And who was Christopher?

Christopher was her boyfriend.

No, no, *Jeff* was her boyfriend. She didn't even know any Christopher.

Christopher! She saw the face clearly in her mind. No longer confused but clear and definite. Yes. Christopher was her boyfriend.

"The name is Jeff, baby," Jeff said. "Get it right." Then he shrugged. "Or hell, call me whatever you want." He slipped his hand beneath the hem of her strangely too-short uniform.

What in the world was she doing here?

"Oh, baby, yes," Jeff moaned.

Aisha shuddered. "What the *hell* do you think you're doing?" she demanded suddenly.

"Nothing yet," Jeff said in a low moan, "but hang on one second—"

The door of the dressing room flew open.

"Get out!" Jeff yelled angrily.

"You BASTARD!" Christopher cried.

"Christopher!" Aisha screamed.

"Christopher?" Jeff repeated, just before Christopher's swinging fist caught him in the jaw.

Nineteen

Claire stepped out of the Z-iosk back into the flow of airport pedestrians rushing to and from their planes. She straightened her clothes as best she could and scooped her hair back over one shoulder.

For a moment she considered just walking away. It would certainly be the easier thing to do. Easier by far. And yet, she told herself that whatever else she might be, she was no coward.

She walked back to the restaurant, past the harassed hostess to the table where the fat guy sat, no longer mumbling over his book but sitting, watching her come near with an expression of mixed triumph and sorrow.

Claire stopped at his table. She looked down at him. He was not in any way attractive. Probably a hundred pounds overweight. His complexion had a greasy, pallid look. His eyes, while bright and alert, were nearly swallowed by his cheeks and his heavy brow.

"Hello, Sean," Claire said.

"Hello, Claire," he said. "Would you like to have a seat?"

Claire pulled out a chair and sat down.

"How did you figure it out?" Sean asked.

Claire pursed her lips thoughtfully. "I guess it was

162

the words. I know the way you express yourself. I know the way you use words.''

Sean nodded, looking gratified, though that expression barely touched the more profound underlying unhappiness. ''You understand how I did it, I suppose?''

''Yes. The hearing aid. It's a receiver.''

''And a transmitter,'' Sean said. ''I could hear everything you said and tell Dennis . . . that's his name, by the way, how to respond.''

''I noticed the hesitation when he talked. And I saw you looking like you were moving your lips reading your book. I think I understand *how*. I don't understand *why*.''

''You don't?'' Sean smiled faintly and met her gaze. ''You really don't?''

Claire looked away, embarrassed.

''I assumed all the time when we talked on the computer that you were . . . I suppose, plain. I had pictured you as a girl who might be as much a victim of her looks as I am of mine. It didn't matter to me what you looked like. I loved your intelligence, your sense of humor, your introspection. When you told me things that made me see you as ruthless, self-serving, Claire, I thought well, she's just an unattractive girl fighting back against a world that isn't prepared to look beneath the surface.''

''I never lied to you about that,'' Claire said. ''I never said I was . . . unattractive.''

''No, you just said how little looks mattered to you.'' Sean laughed bitterly. ''People who say that usually say it because they've been on the wrong end of the looks war. People like me say it.''

''So, why Dennis?''

''It occurred to me, quite late really, that there was one other group of people who went around pretending looks didn't matter. People like you. This terrible fear grew . . . a fear that maybe you weren't at all what I thought you were. And so, it being Halloween—"

"You arranged to wear a mask," Claire said.

"A mask. Yes. A Halloween mask that would make me as handsome as any girl could want. I hoped, I even convinced myself that, it was silly, that I had brought Dennis with me for no reason. I told myself I was being stupid. I told myself that no matter what you looked like, *you* would be able to see beneath . . . this." He held out his hands in a gesture that presented his vast bulk.

"Maybe I would have," Claire said. "You didn't give me the chance."

"No, I didn't," Sean admitted softly. "I saw you as you arrived. A girl of the right age, alone, not carrying luggage. I knew it was you. You stopped my heart, Claire. You were this vision of perfect beauty, of elegance, of confidence. Everything I could never be, and everything I could never have. All my courage evaporated. *I* couldn't talk to a girl like you. Not *me*. So I told Dennis he was on." Sean managed a ruined smile. "He wants to be an actor. I'm sorry he got a little carried away. *That* was never part of my plan."

"I might have surprised you, Sean," Claire said. "I'm really not superficial. I'm really not obsessed with looks. I'm really not one of those girls."

"Remember when Dennis got up to go to the men's room?" Sean asked. "Remember the way you followed him with your eyes? And then when your gaze drifted over to me?"

"Yes," Claire admitted. Yes, she remembered.

"I've seen that look before, Claire. The way the curtain comes down, the face goes blank, the eyes drift away indifferently. The way your lips curled with just the hint of a sneer. The look that says 'don't even bother to dream about it, fat boy.' "

Claire felt her face flush. Yes, this was the real Sean.

The perceptive, intelligent Sean she had come to know. And yet had not known.

"Someday," he said gently, "a girl will come along, and I *really* don't care what she looks like, who will care more about what is in my mind, and my heart . . ." His voice tripped at the word *heart*. In a ragged whisper he went on. "A girl who will care more about what's in my heart than how I look."

"Sean . . . Sean . . ." Claire couldn't think of anything more to say.

His eyes were wet, but his gaze met hers, unflinching. "Are you that girl, Claire? Are you the girl who can love me for what I am inside? Not *like* a brother, or a pal. You know what I mean."

Am I? Claire wondered. *Am I, really? Or am I as cruel to people like Sean as everyone else in the world?*

"I, uh, have to go to the men's room," Sean said. He levered himself heavily up out of his chair. He tucked the tail of his shirt back in his pants. "Do me a favor, Claire. Be honest, okay? And if you are *not* the girl I'm talking about, then please, don't be here when I get back, all right?"

Jake ran from Lara's apartment like he was being chased. He ran along rain-glistening cobblestones painted with reflected neon. He dodged slow-crawling cars squeezing their way through the narrow Portside Weymouth streets. He ran until he was gasping for breath among the gloomy, darkened warehouses of the waterfront. Ran away from the lights, and into the darkness.

The beer had taken a toll on his stamina that even the adrenaline of terror couldn't overcome. He sagged against a loading platform that smelled of the urine of earlier drunks, watched by the glittering eyes of a cat on the hunt.

165

Lara had done it deliberately, of that he was certain. Lara was insane or perhaps just evil. She had known about Wade and had made his name come up on the Ouija board. Lots of people still remembered Wade. Lots of people knew Jake's big brother had died. Why Lara had wanted to frighten him Jake couldn't guess, but he knew one thing: it had been a fake. Spirits didn't speak through Ouija boards. It was ridiculous. And anyway, Wade was in heaven. He wasn't some disconnected spirit wandering around waiting for Benjamin and Zoey's drunken, probably crazy half sister to call him up.

Jake felt as if his skin was crawling. He scratched viciously at his arms and shoulders. Like ants on his skin. The damp, that's what it was. The clamminess of the rain that made his clothing stick to him.

He looked up and saw a bright light. Neon and fluorescence, a block away. A lone beacon of brightness in this grubby neighborhood of abandoned buildings, parking lots, and warehouses.

He pushed away from the loading platform, trying as he walked to steady his breathing. He was an athlete, after all. He was in better shape than this. A few beers couldn't throw him this far off.

He walked fast, suddenly uncomfortable among the shadows, wishing he had stayed among the brighter lights of Portside. Nothing bad could happen over there, amid the expensive restaurants and overpriced tourist shops. But he was drawn not back to Portside but toward the rapidly growing light, now just a few hundred yards away. He could read the individual beer signs in the windows. Budweiser. Bass Ale. Miller.

Where had this liquor store come from? It had to be new. He'd never noticed it in this area before, certainly. And wouldn't he have noticed?

He knew he probably shouldn't drink any more. But his nerves were a wreck. The fault of that crazy bitch and her crazier ideas. Her father a devil! Good Lord. Had the girl thought about Prozac? She needed professional help.

Jake giggled, then laughed, loud and defiant. "Crazy damned bitch!" he yelled up at the night sky.

Yes, a drink would calm his nerves right down. Then he'd head on back to the island. Just get calmed down, and then straight home.

He opened the glass door of the store. The brilliance of the light, reflected back by a thousand glass bottles, made him squint and cover his eyes. He was the only person in the store except for a redheaded, middle-aged woman chain-smoking behind the counter. She leered at him as he came in.

"Tough night, honey?" she asked.

"Yeah. It's raining," Jake said. He went to the tequila section, grabbing a fifth of Cuervo Gold. He carried it defiantly back to the woman.

"I'll need to see some ID," she said around her cigarette.

Jake felt a chill. Wade's driver's license.

He stared at the bottle. He looked at the woman. She grinned back. Cigarette smoke rose from her, for a moment giving Jake the eerie sense that she herself was smoldering.

Wade's license. He reached reluctantly back and pulled it from his pocket.

He slid it across the counter. The woman glanced down at it and gave him a grin. "That's it," she said. "That's it."

Jake threw damp, crumpled bills on the counter and grabbed the bottle. Outside it was dark and welcoming. He started away, plunging into the nearest shadow. There he twisted the cap off the bottle and raised it high, draining a quarter of the liquid fire down his throat.

"Oh, man, that's better. That is *so* much better."

He set off aimlessly, staying to dark streets, sidling away from the rare passing cars. Moving to avoid the chance of being intercepted by a cop who might take his bottle away.

He took a new drink every few minutes, and soon he was staggering in a way that struck him as amazingly funny. The more he drank the more he staggered and the more he laughed, roaring at lampposts and fire hydrants.

It surprised him when he looked down and saw that the pavement had become grass. He glared around him, laboring to focus his eyes. They focused on a cold, white angel.

"Ahh!" he cried. Then, focusing more carefully, he saw that the angel was just a marble figure. A statuette atop an elaborate tombstone.

He was in the graveyard.

He spun around. Everywhere, the moonlit markers. Everywhere, chiseled in marble, the names of the dead.

Jake wanted to run, tried to run, but his feet tangled and he fell, hands and knees in the wet grass. The bottle! It had rolled away and he felt around for it, nearly crying with relief when his hands touched it.

Jake snuggled the bottle close and sat back against a tombstone.

And then, without turning to look, he knew. With a dread that soaked through to his bones, he knew the name on the tombstone.

Twenty

"There! Lights!" Nina cried.

"Where?" Benjamin yelled.

"There are lights through the woods. Lots, like fire or something!" Nina cried. They had gotten away from the farmer's barn, but it was still all too close. Nina had wanted to run for the van, but Benjamin had pointed out that it was stuck, and it would be the first place the murderous, psychopathic farmer would look for them. So they had taken off across the muddy field, panic-stricken, babbling like idiots, racing at top speed without any idea where they were going.

Now, looking anxiously back, Nina could still see the single light of the farmhouse. And looking ahead, she saw flickering firelight just within the nearby woods.

"Hey, maybe it's a campground," Benjamin said excitedly. "You said fire."

"Yes. That must be it!" Nina cried. They were both talking in slightly hysterical whispers and panting heavily. Running through mud was exhausting. Benjamin still carried the pitchfork in his free hand. It made a strange contrast with his mud-spattered, red silk tuxedo. But fashion statements were the last thing they needed to worry about.

"The old man said there were strange things in these

woods on Halloween night," Benjamin cautioned.

"Yeah! Him and his damned dog," Nina said. "Come on."

She led the way as quickly as she could across the mud, muttering the whole time under her breath. "Campers. Campers are always nice people. Probably make us hot chocolate. Over there, roasting marshmallows and having sing-alongs." Nina paused to consider. They *were* having a sing-along.

"Yeah, I hear it," Benjamin said without being asked. "It sounds like religious singing of some kind. They're so off-key I can't be sure."

"Religious music?"

"Sure. Hey, they're probably like some church group on a camp-out."

"Exactly," Nina agreed. "Church groups are always camping out and singing 'Kumbaya' around the fire." She felt at least the sharper edges of terror recede. They would reach the campers in a few minutes. And so far, there was no sign that the psycho farmer or his psycho dog was following them.

They slogged along enthusiastically and reached the first trees. "I can see them better now," Nina said. "Big bonfire and people dancing."

"I still don't get the music, though," Benjamin said. "It sounds kind of old. Like, I don't know, like out of the Middle Ages almost."

"Who cares what kind of music they like?" Nina said, exasperated now that safety was at hand. "Like we should go off and look for people with better taste in music?"

The fire was in a clearing. It wasn't until Nina and Benjamin emerged into that clearing that Nina noticed something odd. There were people dancing around the bonfire, all right. People wearing nothing but gauzy, flowing garments. Some had body parts painted with broad slashes of color. And on their heads, huge masks. Goats, from the look of them. Great, elaborate goat heads with exaggerated horns.

"Benjamin." Nina tried to flatten the terror that was urging her to scream. "Benjamin, there are half-naked people dancing around with these big goat masks on their heads."

"Huh?"

"Oh, my God," Nina said in an awed whisper.

"Oh, my God," Benjamin repeated. "It's like a . . . like a black mass or something!"

Suddenly from the woods behind them the tramp of heavy boots, crashing toward them. And then, a beastly growl.

"It's the farmer!" Nina screamed. "Run!"

She grabbed Benjamin's arm and ran, tearing through the last few bushes. Nina slipped and fell hard. Benjamin, not knowing where she had gone, ran on several steps.

He emerged into the circle of firelight, waving the pitchfork wildly and screaming, "Down, Moloch, down!"

The singing stopped dead.

Twenty half-naked figures, of both sexes, froze. Stock-still. Staring at him from beneath their elaborate goat masks.

And then one of them screamed. And then others screamed. In blind panic they ran, flinging aside their goat masks as they went, bare legs and painted arms flashing in the firelight.

"What the *hell*?" someone shouted. "What the hell is going on?"

"Nina!" Benjamin cried.

"Benjamin!" Nina ran to him, clutching his arm tightly.

"Kee-rist!" someone yelled in annoyance. "Cut. Cut.

Don, go see if you can round them up again. Delia, you go with him. Tell those idiots . . . tell our guests it's just some kid in a costume.''

From the far side of the fire Nina saw a man emerge. He was wearing a baseball cap and carrying a clipboard. He stopped in front of them, hands on hips. ''I suppose you two think this is funny?''

''Nina, what's going on?'' Benjamin asked.

''What's going on?'' Nina asked the man in the cap.

''Like you don't know.''

''Mister, I promise you, we have absolutely no idea. . . . Our van got stuck in the mud . . . and then this farmer and his dog and . . . We have no idea.''

''None,'' Benjamin agreed.

''It was *supposed* to be an authentic re-creation of a witches' coven, holding their Halloween ceremony,'' the man said. ''You know, like the witches of Salem? Back around 1692? They teach you kids any history in school nowadays?''

''I may have heard something about them,'' Benjamin said.

''Well, it was quite a show. Until you pop up, dressed like the devil and waving a pitchfork.''

''Oh,'' Nina said, feeling confused. Should she still be terrified? This guy didn't seem very frightening.

''You scared them half to death.'' The man allowed a wry smile. ''These people are into doing historic re-creations. Most of them are university kids, so I doubt they believe in any of this nonsense, but then again, I don't think they expected to see someone all dressed in red and carrying a pitchfork show up.''

Nina groaned and covered her face with her hands. ''Um, did they start off with this like, bloodcurdling scream? Like maybe a couple of minutes ago?''

''Well, it sure wasn't me,'' the man said.

''Sorry if we screwed up your ceremony,'' Benjamin

said, clearly fighting an urge to giggle hysterically.

"Not *my* ceremony. I'm just here to get some video on it," the man said. "For the show."

"The show?"

"*Jerry Springer*. Should be on sometime next week. We're having some descendants of some of the original witches of Salem. And these folks . . . these folks you just scared half to death . . . were reenacting what they say was one of the ceremonies that got the witches in trouble."

"I warned you there were some strange things in these woods tonight." The farmer was standing behind them. Moloch panted contentedly.

Nina felt her body sag in relief. In a moment, she knew, the embarrassment would start to set in. But for now she was still enjoying the relief. "Um, let me guess," she said to the farmer. "You didn't murder your wife, right?"

"Murder her? What are you, crazy? She run off with some punk to New York. Electrocuted from a downed power line in 1948, may she rot in hell."

"Come by to bring me flowers, little brother?"

Jake's heart felt as if it was being squeezed by a giant, cold hand. His throat was tight. His hands were trembling so badly that he dropped the bottle. It rolled off his lap and onto the grass.

Jake knew it was just some drunken hallucination. Had to be. And yet . . . it *was* Wade's voice.

He fought the paralyzing terror to slowly raise his head. Yes. Standing there before him, only a few feet away. Just as he had always looked. The same Wade. Only . . . somehow not. Insubstantial. Jake realized he could see the outline of a gravestone behind Wade. Could see it *through* his brother.

"Not going to wet your pants, are you?" Wade sneered.

"You're not real," Jake whispered.

"Oh, I'm real enough."

"You're dead, Wade," Jake said. His voice was like gravel. His teeth were clenched tight.

"Well, yeah, I'm dead. But I don't think you should hold that against me," Wade said.

"This can't happen."

"Sure it can, little brother. It *is* happening."

"Why are you doing this to me?" Jake moaned.

"Me? Jeez, kid. I'm not the one with some explaining to do. Why don't you tell me what you're doing, sitting stinking drunk on my grave?"

Jake felt around on the grass for the bottle. A drink. He had never needed a drink more than right now.

"Yeah," Wade jeered, "reach for the bottle."

Jake found the bottle and put it to his lips. Wade shook his head slowly. "Don't do that, man."

"You did it," Jake said accusingly.

Wade nodded. "I know. But don't *you* do it. You're a drunk, Jake."

Jake managed a sneer. He was getting used to the hallucination now. This figment of his own imagination. "I have plenty of reason to want to get drunk."

Wade smiled sadly. "And there will always be plenty of reason, Jake. Every day you'll be able to find some good excuse. So, soon you'll be drinking every day."

"Maybe so," Jake said. He raised the bottle a second time.

Wade came closer. Without sound, without rustling the grass under his feet, he was closer. He knelt down now, squatting comfortably. "You know, I was a lousy big brother, Jake."

"You were the best," Jake argued gruffly.

"No. You told yourself that because you felt bad over

me dying. But I was a creep to you." He smiled. "No point in b.s.'ing myself now that I'm dead. I was a dick."

Jake shrugged.

"So, I'm glad I have this one opportunity, little brother," Wade said. He reached out a hand to touch Jake's shoulder. Jake felt a cold shudder pass through him. "You have to stop it, man. You have to stop destroying yourself, Jake. Just stop. Because see, if you don't stop trying to kill yourself, little brother, you're going to succeed."

"What are you talking about?" Jake asked, his voice rattling with renewed fear.

"You're on a path, Jake," Wade said. "Stay on that path, man, and a year from now you'll be with me. Right here." Wade patted the grass in the empty space beside his own grave. "Live, Jake. Everyone dies eventually, little brother, but for now, live. Just live."

Twenty-one

The last train had left. There were no more buses. Car rental companies wouldn't rent to a driver under age twenty-one. So Zoey had to wait for Aisha and the two boys to come back to the parking garage and Aisha's car. Zoey stayed inside the tiny, overheated office where the parking lot guard was watching *Night of the Living Dead* on a small black-and-white TV.

She had hoped that she might find the van, her family's van, the one that Nina was supposed to have driven down with Benjamin. But no van. No Nina. No Benjamin.

Zoey worried a little over what might have happened to Nina and Benjamin, but decided they would most likely be fine. Nina could see, and Benjamin could think. Between them they made one fully responsible, capable person.

After a while Zoey spotted Aisha, Christopher, and Lucas coming down the street. Lucas. She looked at him with all the hatred she could summon.

She would never forgive him. Never.

Claire waited a full minute after Sean left the table. She wanted to wait for him to come back. She wanted to show him that she *was* the girl he had hoped she would be.

But that would be a lie. And giving him false hope would be too cruel, by far. She still believed in her heart that she wasn't a person who cared about looks. That she wasn't prejudiced, unable to see beneath the surface.

And yet, she would never be what Sean wanted. That was the truth. He hadn't realized it yet, but his image of her was of a person whose faults were understandable, acceptable, because she was fighting back against a world that mistreated her.

But Claire knew she was no victim. She had been given everything the world could give. She had no excuses. And when Sean understood that, the truth would be clear: it wasn't that *he* was somehow not good enough for her. She would be doing him a favor, leaving him now.

Or perhaps she was just rationalizing, Claire told herself. Yes, that was more likely, wasn't it?

So Claire got up and walked away, a beautiful, elegant girl, ignoring the tears that streamed down her face. And by the time she had reached her car, she was composed again.

She drove back toward home and with all her will-power, resisted the picture of Sean, sweet, smart, thoughtful Sean, coming back out to find her gone.

Gone as he had known in his heart that she would be.

"Okay," Nina said. "Anyone asks, we ran out of gas."

"Ran out of gas," Benjamin concurred. A guy from the *Jerry Springer* crew had helped push the van out of the mud. Benjamin had retrieved his clothing from the farmer's barn. He had left the pitchfork where he had found it.

"Silly us, we never even thought to check the gas gauge."

"Exactly," Benjamin said. "We certainly did not get lost on a back road, decide that an old farmer was a mass-murdering Freddy Kreuger clone, and run in terror from a howling dog, with the result that I burst into the middle of a black mass, dressed as Satan, carrying a pitchfork, and screaming 'down, Moloch, down' at the top of my lungs."

"Nope. That certainly never happened. Because, see, if we told people that, then we'd look like idiots," Nina said.

"Ran out of gas."

"No gas."

"Not a drop."

"Temporary amnesia," Christopher said, savoring the phrase yet again, with the same vengeful malice. He was driving the car. Aisha was sitting sullenly in the back alongside an equally sullen Zoey. Lucas was in the passenger seat, staring out into the black night. "Temporary amnesia. Oh, yes."

"It happens to be the truth," Aisha mumbled.

"Your purse is snatched and somehow, as a result of this, you end up in this guy's dressing room about two seconds away from doing with *him* what you flat refuse to do with me."

"I told you, Christopher, it's more complicated than that," Aisha said.

"Oh, yeah. Complications. Complications." He nodded grimly. "They better be some really great complications. Temporary amnesia! Thought she was fourteen again."

Aisha rolled her eyes. Okay, it *was* a little hard to believe. But Christopher should be more understanding. If the situation were reversed . . . bad example. If it were

Christopher telling *her* this story, she'd have killed him by now.

Plus, Christopher hadn't walked away pouting when he'd seen her in an embarrassing position with Jeff. He'd come rushing in to save her. Which was really pretty sweet.

She leaned forward and put her arms around Christopher's neck. She nuzzled his neck and kissed his earlobe.

"Trying to make up, huh?" he grumbled.

"Yes," Aisha said. She kissed the side of his neck again and rested her head on his shoulder. "I love you, Christopher," she whispered.

He stared ahead stonily for about fifteen seconds. Then, "Okay, Lucas, your turn to drive. I can't drive and make up at the same time."

They arrived home in separate groups, spread across the night. Aisha, Christopher, Zoey, and Lucas made it back to Weymouth a little after midnight and caught the water ferry home, splitting the cost four ways. The trip across to the island was spent with Aisha and Christopher in quiet conversation as Aisha told Christopher more details. Not *all* the details, but at least the important ones.

Later that night Aisha went around with Christopher, helping him deliver the morning papers in his pathetically beat-up island car.

Zoey and Lucas didn't speak on the trip over. Simple geography required them to walk in the same direction from the ferry landing to their homes, but Zoey pointedly stayed ahead of him and didn't look back.

Benjamin and Nina arrived back at three in the morning, exhausted but in good spirits. They caught the water taxi and charged it to Nina's father on the grounds that, after all, he was rich.

Claire drove for many hours after leaving Sean in the airport. She had driven down from Boston to Cape Cod, restless and too far gone in thought to feel sleepy. At last, she had turned back north. She arrived back in Weymouth and parked the Mercedes in the parking garage, just as the city was waking up to a gray dawn and the first day of November.

She had a light breakfast in a diner and decided against going home at all. It was a school day, after all. She didn't have her books, and she was overdressed for a day of high school, but she didn't much care if people wondered what she was doing in heels and a silk blouse. Claire had never worried much how she looked.

Jake woke up in the graveyard just before dawn. His head was splitting. He was half-frozen and stiff. His mouth felt like he'd been eating dirt. His throat was raw, his stomach ravaged. He saw the half-full bottle of tequila lying on the grass.

The hair of the dog, as the saying went. That's what he needed: a good, stiff drink to kill the pain of the hangover. Right.

He lifted the bottle and without hesitation emptied the contents out over his brother's grave. He staggered to school long before it was open. He had a key to the gym, let himself in, and slept for two hours in the locker room. Then he drank a quart of water and, fighting the agonizing pain in every fiber of his body, put himself through an hour of calisthenics, sweating the last of the alcohol out of his body.

"Oh, no," Zoey moaned. "No way."

The alarm had gone off way too early. She'd barely closed her eyes. As exhausted as she had been, she'd not been able to fall asleep. Instead she had tossed and turned, pursuing bitter, resentful thoughts. Wallowing in anger. Unable to turn off the images of Lucas with

180

Claire. Unable to separate them in her mind from the devastating images of her mother with Mr. McRoyan. No more capable of forgiving Lucas than her father was capable of forgiving her mother. And not wanting to try.

She swiped angrily at the alarm and reluctantly threw back the covers. The Boston Bruins jersey she slept in was twisted around, and she twisted it back. Then she stubbed her toe on the corner of her dresser and let loose a string of violent curses. What a wonderful start to the day. Another stinking, rotten day.

Her gaze swept angrily around her room. She was tired of it. Sick of it. The walls felt like they were closing in. The ceiling, slanting low in the corners, made her feel claustrophobic. Not too many more months and she would be on her way to college, and good riddance to this house, and her parents, and this tiny, tiresome island and its tiresome people. When she got away from Chatham Island, she would stay gone. And when she was off at college, finally she would no longer give a damn about Lucas.

She was trembling with anger still. Anger and weariness and resentment at her parents, at her supposed friend Claire, even at Benjamin for not being there last night and for being so contemptibly happy when her entire life was falling apart.

She drew on a robe and went downstairs. Coffee. She needed coffee, even before she showered. She found Benjamin in the kitchen, drinking a cup. He smiled at her.

"Oh, here you are," Zoey sneered. "Where were you last night? Didn't it occur to you that I might be worried?"

"Sorry, *Mom*," Benjamin said complacently. "The van ran out of gas."

"Don't call me Mom," Zoey snapped. "I consider that an insult."

Benjamin tilted his head quizzically. "PMS? Or are you just being an unholy bitch for no reason?"

"Benjamin, you know something? I don't really like—" She stopped, listening. A noise from upstairs. A low voice. A man's voice. Zoey slammed her cup down on the table, making Benjamin jump. "Damn it, does she have that man here in our own house?"

"Zoey, jeez, get a grip," Benjamin said, annoyed now. "If you want to know—"

"Don't you condescend to me!" Zoey yelled. "I know what's going on, and I'm not going to put up with it." She spun on her heel and raced for the stairs.

"Zoey, don't—" Benjamin yelled after her.

But Zoey was beyond listening. If her mother thought she could have her *boyfriend* spend the night like it was perfectly normal, well, she was going to find out differently. Zoey ran up the stairs, bristling with all the rage that had built up in the last few weeks.

She reached her mother's door. Yes, a male voice, murmuring inside. Incredible! Zoey pounded with her fist on the door. She snatched at the handle and threw it open, already loading up the cry of outrage.

And there she was. Her mother, just hastily pulling on her robe. And the man—

The man. Her father.

"Daddy?"

Her father looked embarrassed. Fortunately he was dressed in his old flannel robe, having been quicker than Zoey's mother.

"Did you want something?" her mother asked pointedly.

"What are you doing here?" Zoey asked her father.

Mr. Passmore smiled sheepishly. "Well . . ."

"He lives here," Zoey's mother said quietly.

"After what . . . after all the things that happened?" Zoey asked, absolutely astonished.

Her father looked at her mother. Zoey saw the way their eyes met. She saw that there were tears in her mother's eyes. Mr. Passmore shrugged, and shook his head slowly. "We've gotten past all that."

"Past it? How could you forgive her after what she did?"

"She forgave me," her father said. "And I forgave her." He shrugged again. "It's what you do when you love someone, Zoey."

Benjamin was looking wonderfully amused as Zoey reentered the kitchen. "I hope they were dressed, at least," he said. "Seeing your parents naked, that's worth like an extra year in therapy."

"They forgave each other," Zoey said blankly. "That's what Daddy told me. Just like that."

Benjamin nodded. "Yeah, I thought all along that's what would happen eventually."

"You thought so?"

"Sure. They're in love, Zoey. Man, I would have thought you of all people could have seen that. Don't you know that love conquers all?" he asked ironically. "Where have *you* been?"

Zoey retrieved her coffee and went to the kitchen window. She sensed eyes watching her and looked up, knowing what she would see. Lucas was standing at the railing of his deck, looking sadly down at her.

Zoey sighed. She went to the telephone and carried it back to the window. She dialed and waited.

Lucas disappeared for a moment, then came back into view carrying a portable phone. He *was* awfully cute, and awfully sweet, and awfully sexy, even if sometimes he had the potential to be slightly a *pig*.

But she did love him, and she had it on good authority that when you loved someone, you forgave.

"You're a jerk, Lucas, and I hate your guts," she said

into the phone, looking up at him. "Unfortunately, I also love you."

She cut the connection before he could answer. But she saw his lips form the three magic words. *I love you.*

"That was sweet," Benjamin said.

"Yeah. You happy now?" Zoey demanded.

"Are you?"

Her parents came down the stairs, looking sheepish. Lucas still watched her from above, smiling radiantly as the early sunlight hit his face. "Yes, I guess I am," Zoey said.

Making Out:
Zoey Plays Games

Flirtation. Deception. Temptation. What else could it be
but book 9?

Life was bliss for **Zoey** and **Lucas** until **Aaron**
showed up on the island. Now **Aaron** wants **Zoey,**
Claire wants **Aaron,** and **Zoey's** got a secret
that EVERYONE is talking about. How long before
Lucas finds out that...

Zoey
plays
games